Praise For Niqui Stanhope And Her Novels

WHATEVER LOLA WANTS

"Sizzling." —*Romance in Color*

"A definite hit." —*Fallen Angel Reviews*

CHANGING THE RULES

"Romance with a hip attitude . . . steamy sexual tension and exuberant energy." —*Publishers Weekly*

"In this funny, sexy, very contemporary romantic comedy, the rules ultimately bend nicely with satisfactory results for all concerned. This lively, sassy romp has appeal far beyond the targeted African American readership." —*Library Journal*

"Stanhope writes with humor and compassion about young black professionals and their quest for true love." —*Romantic Times*

"The romance is appealing, as fans will like the antics of the lead duo, particularly Marcel." —*Midwest Book Review*

SWEET TEMPTATION

"Readers will fall in love." —*Romantic Times*

MADE FOR EACH OTHER

"Niqui Stanhope has written a riveting story that pulls the reader along on a tide of sensuality, lush scenery, and unforgettable romance." —*Romantic Times*

DISTANT MEMORIES

"*Distant Memories* is a taut, exciting romantic suspense that showcases Ms. Stanhope's unique literary talents . . . the story is a 'must-read.' " —*Romantic Times*

St. Martin's Paperbacks Titles
by Niqui Stanhope

Whatever Lola Wants

Changing the Rules

She's Gotta Have It

Niqui Stanhope

St. Martin's Paperbacks

SHE'S GOTTA HAVE IT

Copyright © 2005 by Niqui Stanhope.

Cover photo © Herman Estevez

ISBN: 0-312-98625-4
EAN: 9780312-98625-4

Printed in the United States of America

St. Martin's Paperbacks edition / August 2005

St. Martin's Paperbacks are published by St. Martin's Press, 175 Fifth Avenue, New York, NY 10010.

10 9 8 7 6 5 4 3 2 1

Thanks for the wonderful music, Oleta Adams. You are one of the most gifted singers around.

Dear Readers,

The Champagne family is back! This time, Nicky Champagne's friend, Harry Britton, runs into a woman who is an even bigger playa than he is! Harry, who has never been dumped in his life, just can't believe it. But Nicky, Gavin, and Summer know that it's nothing but love. There's just one little complication though— they've got to convince Harry of this.

But I won't say any more. I invite you to sit back, relax, and enjoy this latest installment in the Champagne family saga! And don't forget to drop me a line when you're done.

Until the next time,

Niqui

Prologue

Harry Britton pulled open the mesh screen front door and bellowed, "Summer? You home?"

"Of course I'm at home," Summer Stevens-Champagne said, emerging from the kitchen, a badly stained apron wrapped about her waist. "Why wouldn't I be at home? Have you forgotten it's my turn to cook Sunday dinner?" She gave her watch a glance. "And they're all due here in under an hour no less."

A hidden smile flickered in the depths of Harry's eyes. Every month it was exactly the same. Summer's Sunday dinners were legendary in the Champagne family. And no amount of coaxing and talking-to could get her to abandon her efforts in this area, either. Invariably, the entire clan would be treated to a medley of singed meats, hard breads, soggy vegetables, and completely unrecognizable desserts. But everyone soldiered bravely through her dinners because no one had the heart to tell her that in the four years since she had married Gavin

Champagne, her culinary skills had, in fact, not improved at all.

"Isn't Amanda cooking this time?" Harry asked, feigned innocence shining brightly in his eyes.

Summer wiped her hands on her apron. "Nope. Not this week. Besides, it's a good thing anyway. God only knows what the food would be like with the way things are between Amanda and Nicky."

Harry was saved from having to respond to this comment on the state of his best friend's marriage by Summer's sudden cry of, "Mother Champagne, please, leave those pots alone."

Summer rushed back toward the kitchen muttering beneath her breath about having altogether too much to contend with today. Harry considered following her for an instant but then decided that it was probably wiser to allow Summer to handle her fractious mother-in-law on her own. His gaze swept the beautifully appointed sitting room with its overstuffed aqua and white sofas and elegant black lacquer tables. He didn't have an eye for interior design or that sort of thing at all, but even he would admit that Summer had done a spectacular job with the house. And with a very active four-year-old boy to keep an eye on, that was surely no easy feat.

Harry wandered out to one of the sweeping verandas and gazed squinty eyed at the bright blue Caribbean Sea. Although it was well after four o'clock in the afternoon, the heat of the day had not yet burned itself off. It gathered on the coconut palms, bringing a bristle of green to their fronds. And it settled right between Harry's brows, causing the smooth skin there to go into an immediate furrow.

He wiped the round of his forehead with the back of a hand. One of these days, not any time soon of course, but one of these days, he was going to buy a piece of land just like the Champagnes had here at Champagne Cove. Maybe it would be on the ocean, maybe not. But it would be big, with lots of fruit trees and more than enough room for kids to play. Lots of kids. Five or six of them. Maybe.

He was so deep in thought that when Summer said, "Five or six of what?" directly behind him, he was not fully prepared to give her his typical smooth "Harry Britton, playboy extraordinaire," light-hearted response. Instead he barely managed a distracted, "What was that?" It had completely escaped his notice that he had spoken any of his thoughts aloud.

Summer propped her hands on her hips and gave him a suspicious golden-eyed look. She knew Harry Britton well, and to her way of thinking, if he was talking about five or six of anything, it was nothing more profound than the fact that he was considering bedding five or six women. And quite probably bedding them all within the next few hours.

"Don't give me that wide-eyed innocent look, Harry Britton," she said, wagging a finger at him. "I heard what you said, and this time I mean it. Don't even think of trying anything with *any* of my cousins. Those three girls are nice, sheltered, religious girls. They've all grown up in the Church. So, they're definitely not the type you're accustomed to . . . to . . . meddling with." She drew a breath and then charged on. "I had a feeling that was why you showed up here so early."

Harry attempted to explain with, "But Nicky asked me to look in on you to make sure—"

She cut him off with a, "'But Nicky' nothing. I know what the two of you are probably planning. And I'm telling you now, I'm not going to stand for it. Not this time. I'm only going to say this to you once. These girls are my cousins. They have never visited Jamaica before. And I would like to return them all to the U.S. in the same untouched condition that they arrived here in. I promised their mother I'd take good care of them. So that means that they are completely off-limits to you. Do you understand what I'm saying?" Her nostrils developed a pretty little flare on either side of the bridge of her nose as she gave him a fierce lioness-with-cubs look.

Harry was tempted to say, "Yes, ma'am," but decided that under the circumstances, those two words might just succeed in bringing her already simmering temper to a complete and irreversible boil. "You can count on me," he said instead.

Summer gave him a considered, "Hmm. I mean it, Harry."

Harry smiled at her. "Trust me, beautiful. I only play with women who already know the game."

Summer's brows smoothed a bit. "Promise me."

Harry folded both arms across his chest and gave Summer a glinting satin-eyed look that worried her all the more.

"I promise."

Chapter One

Hedonism III was simply one of the most extraordinary resorts Camille Roberts had ever seen. It wrapped itself around the glittering blue shoreline of the north coast of Jamaica in the most amazing way. And as she climbed from the low-slung limousine, brown legs long, toned, and very bare, she actually felt a trifle overdressed in her bright yellow polka-dot mini, black tank top, and wide-brimmed yellow straw hat. Her eyes ran in appreciation over the young Adonis who had opened the car door for her. He was a gorgeous specimen of manhood; there was no doubt about that. He stood at least six feet tall. Was well muscled in all of the right places. Had a flat washboard stomach with a beautiful six-pack of muscles. And was chocolate brown in complexion and G-stringed, with no other garment to adorn his body but a crisp little bow tie about his neck.

A playful impulse ran through Camille, and as she walked past him and into the hotel she asked in a soft undertone, "Is that all you usually wear?"

The Adonis smiled and responded in kind, "Only during the day, ma'am." And he winked at her in a manner that told Camille that should she suggest a little rendezvous later in the evening, he would be more than willing to oblige her. But even though she had flown to Jamaica on her girlfriend Lola's private jet with the very intention of seeking out and bedding a sexy young thing, this man held no real interest for her. The one she would choose would be just as sexy but much more special. And she would know him as soon as she saw him.

"This way please, ma'am." Another scantily dressed man smiled. "Your suite is ready for you."

A sigh of utter contentment drifted from between Camille's lips. Now, this was exactly what she needed. A weekend away from the crazy hurly-burly of planning a wedding. If all went according to plan, in just about eight weeks she would be Mrs. Anthony Davis. And she thanked the heavens above that she had finally found exactly the right kind of man. Wealthy. Older. Generous. He would pamper her well. And she would thoroughly enjoy her new life. So what if her husband-to-be could not satisfy her in bed? She had had more than enough sex in her life so far to make up for that little problem. Besides, if ever the strain of it all became too much for her . . . well, that was another matter entirely. She would have to think about that. Because she was not the sort of woman who took the taking of a lover lightly. Some aspects of marriage were still sacred to her. And fooling around once she had tied the knot was not something that she was willing to do. Hence the reason for her weekend trip to Jamaica. She was going to do all of her fooling around now, while she still could.

She nodded and smiled at another member of the hotel staff. The tangy salty smell of the navy blue Caribbean sea perfumed the air, and it made her feel randy, randy for just about anything. She had brought a weekend bag of party things with her. Frilly, lacy, silky garments with suggestive bows and convenient ties. She had also packed a black lace mask as an afterthought, but now she was glad she had decided to bring it along. Because . . . it would be just the thing. Just the thing to use once she found that one special man.

"Harry!" Summer bellowed from somewhere on the second floor of the house.

Harry Britton, who was at that very moment up to his elbows in a sink full of soapsuds, wiped his hands hurriedly on the thick towel hanging from the handle of the fridge and then sprinted in the direction of her voice. God Almighty, what was going on? Was she being attacked?

He took the stairs two at a time and very nearly knocked Summer down as he rounded the corner.

"Why are you charging about the place like a mad bull, for heaven's sake?" Summer asked as soon as she had managed to get her breath back.

"You screamed, so naturally I thought . . ."

"I did not scream," Summer said with a great degree of patience. "I was just trying to tell you that they're coming. Gavin just called from the car. They're not ten minutes away." And she switched conversational streams as fluidly as she always did. "I'm going to finish dressing, so . . . is the table ready? Everything nicely laid out? Knives? Forks? Plates? Everything?"

Harry nodded in a good-natured manner and said, "Check. Check. And check again, ma'am. Everything's done."

"Did you remember to wash the big silver bowl? The one for the stew?"

"I washed that one, as well as the big soup tureen."

Summer's brow furrowed. "Soup tureen? We're not having any soup today."

Harry bit on the side of his mouth and struggled valiantly against the chuckle brewing in his chest. No soup? So what in the name of heaven was that concoction that was even now simmering on the stove?

"Anyway," Summer said, waving away whatever it was Harry was about to say, "I'm going to go and get changed. OK? So, keep an eye on things." And she rolled her eyes. "You know what I mean, right? Don't, under any circumstances, let Mother Champagne add anything to my pots. Last time she just about ruined the food."

Harry coughed and nodded. As far as he was concerned, the Sunday dinner that Summer had cooked last month had been ruined long before Mother Champagne had gotten her hands on it. But he wisely kept such thoughts to himself and instead said, "I'll keep an eye on things. Don't you worry."

Summer gave him a grateful smile and a slightly apologetic, "You're such a nice guy, Harry Britton. I'm sorry I yelled at you before. But stay away from those girls, though . . ." She wagged a finger at him. "I mean it." And before he could say much of anything in reply, she said, "I'm going to get dressed."

Chapter Two

Camille groaned in delight as several broad blunt-tipped fingers walked their way down the curve of her spine. This was truly heaven indeed. A full-body massage at five o'clock in the evening? A crystal blue ocean directly before her. Soft evening breeze billowing across the veranda, making her skin feel like silk itself. The scent of hibiscus and jasmine in the air. The sound of *Shaggy* drifting sweetly on the wind. Now, what could be better than that?

She turned her head slightly to give the masseur full access to the long length of her neck, and as his fingers moved obligingly, she muttered an encouraging, "Yes, that's it. Right there. That's the spot right there."

The blunt-tipped fingers paused and then went back over the delicate spot. Over and over and over again until Camille thought that she must surely die from all of this pleasure.

She closed her eyes and gave herself up to the feeling. Now this was what she had needed for such

a very long time. This utter and total dedication to
the pursuit of nothing but wicked pleasure. Why had
she denied herself this for so long?

The masseur was blissfully silent as the comfortable minutes ticked by, letting his fingers talk to the
sore muscles in her back, the fine bones in her neck,
the dip and curve of each of her thighs. It was glori-
ous. Like nothing else. And Camille relaxed into the
coziness of her thoughts and dreamily considered
the next sinful item on the agenda.

After the hour-long massage was through, she
would have a chilled champagne-scented bubble
bath. She had asked that the bathtub be lined with
flickering scented candles and that a large dish of
chocolate-dipped strawberries be waiting on the lip
of the large Roman tub. When she was through with
that, she would have a nice long nap on the veranda.
She'd been told that even at nighttime in Jamaica the
temperature fell to nothing lower than a balmy
seventy-five degrees. But feeling the possible chill
of night air was not something that she even had to
worry about, since she would be checked on by her
personal room attendant while she slumbered, and
covered with an appropriate blanket, should she
need it.

She sucked in a delicious breath as the strong fingers stroked her hair apart and moved slowly across
her scalp. Her eyelids fluttered at the feel of them.
This was it. This was the only life she could possibly
live. And no, she wasn't at all sorry that she had de-

cided to marry for money. How could she possibly give any of this up? Work nine to five. Every day up at the crack of dawn to battle traffic and all sorts of crazies? Please. What for? She could only marry a rich man. *A rich man.* The others could just . . . well, they knew what they could do. . . .

"Christ Almighty, what is with this dog?" Nicholas Champagne said in frustration as the brown-haired dog of indeterminate pedigree attempted to hump his leg for the third consecutive time.

He pushed the animal away with the side of his foot and Amanda Champagne pressed her lips together and tried not to laugh. She didn't want her husband to see even the trace of a smile on her lips. She was very upset with him at the moment, and no amount of unsolicited humping by a poor deranged dog would make her forget it.

"Good God. And it's a girl, too. Summer!" Nicholas bellowed.

"Well, that makes a lot of sense," Amanda muttered. Of course it would have to be a female dog. Only a *female* dog would ever hump Nicholas "Ladies' Man" Champagne's leg. It was probably the first female dog in the entire world to do that.

Nicholas gave his wife a glance. She hadn't said a single word to him in the last two hours. Why this was, he had no idea at all. She had been so moody and difficult since they had started trying to get pregnant. Yes, they seemed to be having a little trou-

ble in that area. Yes, they had been trying now for
more than a year with no success at all. But why
should that throw her into a mood at the least little
thing? One minute she could be laughing with him,
and the next she was upset just because he might
have smiled at a waitress or some other inconse-
quential person. Women. He would never understand them.

"Summer!" he shouted again as the dog made another go at his leg.

The screen door pushed open and Harry loomed
big and large in the doorway. He was dressed in a
huge grin and a water-stained apron.

"So, you finally decided to show up, huh?
Amanda, sweetheart, you look wonderful," he said
with a playful glance in her direction.

Amanda brushed by him and entered the house
with a "You men are all the same" comment hanging in the air.

Harry exchanged a glance with Nicholas.
"What'd I say?"

Nicholas shrugged. "It's this baby thing. It's driving her crazy. And . . ." He paused to give the dog a
gentle shove yet again. "Look, there're some
desserts and things in the car, but I can't chance
bringing them out with this crazy dog attacking my
legs at every turn. See if you can hold on to her while
I . . . Where are Gavin and the kids?" he asked,
changing conversational directions for a moment.

Harry whipped off the apron and slung it across a

shoulder. "Gone to pick up Summer's cousins at Norman Manley Airport in Kingston."

Nicholas leaned into the black Land Rover as Harry held on to the dog. "I'd forgotten they were coming this week," he said, and gently eased a large nicely iced butter sponge across the leather of the backseat. Once he'd gotten his fingers securely beneath the base of it, he straightened to say, "They're nice girls, I've heard."

Harry grinned and did his best to hold on to the squirming dog. "I've already gotten my marching orders from Summer."

Nicholas laughed. "I should've known she wouldn't mince words with you. Where is she, by the way?"

Amanda, halfway up the stairs to the second floor of the house, was asking the very same question.

"Summer? Where are you hiding? I've got to talk to you before everyone gets here."

"Bedroom," Summer shouted, and then proceeded to wiggle her way into a nicely printed spaghetti-strapped sundress. "The door's open," she called at the sound of a soft tap on the wood.

Amanda pushed open the door and gave Summer a watery smile. "I . . . I brought cake for dessert." She sniffed and wiped a finger beneath her nose. "And a couple of cobblers. Peach. Thick crumbly crust. The way you like it."

Summer paused in her struggle to straighten the dress across her hips and said in a questioning voice, "Mandy?" And then with a distinct note of worry as a tear traced its way down one side of Amanda's face, "Mandy. What's the matter? Why are you crying?"

Amanda wiped the side of her face dry and then said in a tight little voice, "It's Nicholas."

Summer held on to a sigh and went to sit on the edge of the large four-poster bed. Nicky again. What was her beautiful brother-in-law doing? He'd married Amanda Drake about three years before, but he still appeared to have little idea as to how to make his marriage work. If it wasn't one thing, it was another.

Summer patted the bed beside her and said in a coaxing manner, "What's that Nicky done now?"

Amanda struggled with another sob and then managed a sodden, "I think he's having an affair . . . or something."

Summer blinked clear golden eyes at her. "An affair? Nicky having an affair? No. He wouldn't do that. I know he was kinda wild before you met him. But as soon as he saw you . . . that was the end of all other women for him."

Amanda shook her head. "Not true. You just don't know."

Summer took her by the shoulders. "But I do know. From the very first time he saw you at my wedding, he . . . he couldn't take his eyes off you. And even after you handcuffed him to that bed and left him there without any keys to free himself with."

Amanda gasped. "He told you about that?"

Summer gave her a patient look. "You've always known that Nicky and I were close. We're like brother and sister, really." She tilted Amanda's face up and wiped away the trace of another tear. "That's why I know for sure. For *sure*. That he's not having an affair. Why would you even think a thing like that?"

"Because—" A knock on the door halted the words in her throat.

Summer sucked in a breath. "Nicky, if that's you, go away. I can't talk to you now."

"It's Harry," came the rumble from behind the door.

"Can't talk to you now, either," Summer shouted. "Mandy and I are having a gossip."

Harry stepped back from the door. In his experience, it was never a good sign when two wives were sequestered in a bedroom, having a "gossip." It almost always meant one thing and one thing only. Trouble. And it didn't take a genius to figure out who it was in the thick of the mess.

"Nick, my friend," Harry said as he walked back into the kitchen, pulled out a stool, and sat. "I think we'd better leave the women alone for a while."

Nicholas straightened from the meat that was sizzling in a pan full of oil. "Did you tell her that the roast is burnt? . . . And raw," he added, giving the piece of meat a poke with the teeth of a long metal fork.

Harry raised his eyebrows. "I think you'd better turn off the oven and go buy your wife some flowers, or candy."

Nicholas scratched the side of his head. "Did she say something to you?"

Harry shrugged. "She and Summer are having 'a gossip' upstairs."

Nicholas sighed. "Sometimes I have to wonder about this whole getting-married thing. One woman for the rest of your life. It just doesn't seem natural."

Harry nodded. "Better you than me. You know how I feel about all of that. No woman's going to tie me down. At least not until I'm close to fifty-five, sixty. By then I'll probably be ready to settle with one woman. A sexy young thing with breasts the size of melons." He laughed at his own joke and then gave his friend a steady-eyed look. "Are you stepping out on her?"

Nicholas paused in his inspection of the pot of soggy corn rice. "Are you kidding me? That woman would kill me in my sleep. Besides, other women just don't seem to do it for me anymore."

Harry laughed in a rueful manner. "God, I'm glad I don't have your problems. So why don't you take your wife away somewhere? A few days in New York. A couple of Broadway shows. A day of shopping on Fifth Avenue. You know, do it up right. Wine.

Roses. Music. Good food. Lots of romance. The whole nine. You know how women like that kind of thing. She'll be purring like a kitten by the time you bring her back."

"Hmm," Nicholas agreed. "Amber's still in school, though. We can't just up and leave her like that. She's—"

"Come on, man," Harry interrupted. "Leave the child with Summer and Gavin. You know they're practically her second parents. Besides, Amber and Adam will have a ball together. I've never seen two kids so much alike."

Nicholas laughed. "Those two? From one day to the next, I never know what they're going to get into. And I'm not sure which one is worse."

He was about to say more on the subject, but his train of thought was suddenly broken by the honking of a car horn.

"That'll be Gavin and the gang," Harry said, standing. "I think, given my little talk with Summer, I'd better hang back a bit until those girls have settled in."

Nicholas chuckled and clapped Harry on the shoulder. "Wise man."

Chapter Three

Gavin Champagne stepped out of the Lexus SUV at almost the exact moment that the two side doors burst open.

"Walk. Walk. Don't run, you two," he shouted as two little bodies hurtled from the backseat of the truck, tore down the short pink gravel pathway, and then bounded up the front stairs and into the house.

"Ladies," Gavin said with a rueful little smile, "welcome to Champagne Cove. Sorry about those two little hooligans. God only knows what they'll be up to in about five minutes."

Francine Stevens was the first to exit the vehicle. She was a tall, willowy girl of about nineteen, with short stylishly permed hair, high cheekbones, beautiful burnt almond eyes, and the figure of a sleek high-fashion model.

"Cousin Gavin," she said with a trace of breathlessness in her voice. "Is this where you and Cousin Summer live? In this big place?"

Gavin smiled at her. "There's much more to the

property than just this house. Once you've settled in, Summer will give you a tour. There's another house up that way through the orchard," he said, turning to point. "Your cousin Nick and his wife live there with little Amber. And when my brother Mik and cousin Rob are down from school, they live there, too." He smiled at them again. "There's also a smaller cottage up the beach a stretch, where my mother lives. But Summer will show you everything."

Francine turned and exchanged a look with her sisters. "Come on, twins," she said after a moment more of staring. "Let's help Cousin Gavin with the bags."

Summer opened the front door just then and squealed, "Oh my God," and came clattering down the stairs in very fashionable two-inch-heeled clogs. "Look at you," she said when she was close enough. "I almost don't even recognize any of you at all. You're all so grown-up. Hi, honey." She beamed at her husband before she swept all three girls up in a giant kissing hug.

Gavin stood back with a pleased smile on his face as the women hugged, kissed, oohed, and aahed. He liked nothing better than making his wife happy. And this was the happiest he had seen her in a while.

"Wait a minute. Wait a minute," Summer said after everyone had gotten at least one solid kiss in. "Let me see now." She held one of the twins by the shoulders. "This has to be Deana," she said after a minute.

And the eighteen-year-old with the short natural haircut chuckled in wicked delight. "You never could tell us apart, Cousin Summer. I'm Diana. She's Deana." And Diana pointed to her sister, an identical version of herself in every way, who smiled back happily.

Summer gave the girls a grin. "Now, how could I have gotten that wrong? And of course, this must be Fancy Francy," she said, turning to the older girl who had been standing a bit apart from her two sisters.

Francine gave her cousin a little nod and a smile. "Hardly anyone calls me Fancy now," she said with a laughing note in her voice.

"Well, we'll just have to do something about that then." Summer beamed. And she linked her arms with the girls' and hustled them into the house.

An hour later, everyone was seated at the long and nicely set dinner table. A large dish of soggy corn rice sat in the center of the spread, with surrounding dishes of greens, macaroni and cheese, sweet potatoes, and a burnt and still smoking piece of meat.

Gavin sat at the head of all of this, as was customary, with Summer on his right and his mother on his immediate left. Harry also sat on the left, next to Nicholas and Amanda. The three girls were placed on the right, next to their cousin. And the two children sat at the foot of the table, in the direct line of view of both sets of parents.

"Well," Summer said, clasping her hands before

her. "Isn't this nice? Good family. Good friends. It's just a pity Mik and Rob couldn't come down from school this time. But they'll be here next weekend. Mik's in his final year of residency. He's going to be a doctor, you know." And there were layers of pride in her voice.

Gavin cleared his throat and then raised his glass of sparkling cider. "I think this calls for a toast. Mom, everyone. Let me first say how grateful—"

Esther Champagne, who had until now been observing the proceedings with a certain quiet equanimity, crossed her arms before her and declared in a very reasonable voice, "I'm not eating any of this mess."

Harry's eyes darted to Summer's face, but he held his tongue and allowed Gavin to speak.

"Now Mom," Gavin said with a great degree of patience. "Summer's been cooking all day. And we have guests. The least we can do is—"

"The least we can do? The least we can do?" Esther Champagne interrupted with some amount of heat. "Every month it's the same thing. Sunday dinners. Sunday dinners. And she always wants to cook. But everyone's afraid to say something." And Esther turned to regard Summer with diamond-bright eyes. "And don't look at me all crazy, either. Because it's nothing for me to take off my shoe and—"

"Yes," Gavin interrupted before more could be said about what exactly was going to be done with the shoe. "Mom, I think it's about time for your medication. Isn't it?"

"Medication?" Esther Champagne inquired in a shrill voice. "I'll give you medication. Don't think you're too grown now. Because—"

The ringing of the doorbell cut across what she was saying, and both Summer and Amanda prepared to rise.

"I'll get it," they both said.

Nicholas gave the two children seated at the foot of the table, who were both watching the unfolding scene with hands cupped to their mouths, a "Don't you dare laugh" look and then said in a brisk manner, "I'll get the medication." And he gently and with some amount of skill managed to coax his mother from the table.

Harry stood. "I'll get the door."

Francine Stevens smiled up at him and said nicely, "Need any help?"

Harry gave her his best paternal smile and said, "I've got it."

Summer flicked a glance between them both. "It's probably Nurse Robbins. She went to pick up some things in Ocho Rios. But can you check, Harry?"

Harry smiled at her. He knew exactly what was going through her beautiful head. And she couldn't be more wrong this time. These girls were much too young for his tastes. Besides, even if he had been interested at all, the fact that they were close relatives of the Champagnes made them automatically off-limits. But that was neither here nor there. He had no interest. None at all.

As soon as he was gone, Summer said in a slow hiss of breath, "I don't know what set Mother Champagne off this time. Sometimes . . ." She sucked in a breath and then continued, "Cousin Gavin's mother," and she gave her cousins an apologetic little glance, "is . . . ah . . . not well. She's OK if she takes her medication regularly. But even then, she can sometimes say strange things. She doesn't mean any harm, though." She exchanged a lightning glance with her husband, who had been silent through all of this. "I hope this hasn't upset you any."

"No, no, Cousin Summer," Francine said smoothly. "It's no problem at all. I was actually going to ask you if I could pray for her. We always pray for the older members of our church. We're known for it."

Amanda looked across at Summer as she said, "Oh, how nice of you. Of course you can say a prayer. But let's wait for Cousin Harry."

Harry returned with Nurse Robbins in tow.

"Did she have another episode?" the matronly woman asked.

"Nicky's with her in the sunroom." Summer nodded.

The nurse gave them all a capable smile. "I'll check on them."

And as soon as Harry was again seated, Summer waved the table into action with, "Come on; come on. Fancy's going to say a special prayer for us. So, everyone hold hands. You, too, Adam," she said to the chuckling three-year-old, whose mop of curly black hair and bright golden eyes were so much like her own.

As Francine began a very reverent prayer of entreaty and thanksgiving, Harry bowed his head—and then recoiled with a cry of, "Jesus Christ," as what was clearly a bare foot with five very active toes settled solidly against his groin.

Chapter Four

It was just before 11:00 p.m. when Camille began getting ready. She had spent most of the afternoon and early evening having every care massaged, plucked, and loofahed away. She'd indulged in a wonderful champagne-scented bubble bath. Chocolate-dipped strawberries. A session with the cosmetologist, who had touched up Camille's French manicure and refreshed her perm. And then she had settled down on the windswept veranda just as the first pink of twilight touched the sky, to eat a light supper of crusty Jamaican patties and savory rice and peas. She'd watched the sun set over the blue horizon with a long glass of chilled white wine in her hand. And as night came in its inevitable way, her mind had turned to other things. The masquerade midnight ball. The sexy black teddy that she intended to wear. The stiletto pumps that made her already long legs look even longer. The man who was going to pass this very night between the silk sheets of her bed.

Camille sat at the dressing table and stared at her reflection. She was a beautiful woman. She knew that. Her eyes were black, not dark brown, as would be typical for a woman of her cinnamon brown complexion. Her face had a pleasing oval shape. Her cheekbones were high and spaced just the right distance apart. Her nose was nicely rounded and symmetrical. And her mouth, possibly her best feature, was sculpted yet pouty and full in the way that men preferred. Yes, she could turn a few heads all right.

She drew her shoulder-length black hair up and back, stared at her reflection for a moment longer before deciding that she would wear her hair back in a ponytail. With the mask in place, she would be both mysterious and provocative. Her identity had to be protected at all costs, but at the same time she had to be able to entice the man she selected tonight. Because it would be the last time for many, many years that she would have really good, mind-blowing sex. And she was going to make the most of it. She was going to ride her mister wonderful until the sun came up, and then and only then would she send him on his way.

She walked across to the large walk-in closet, a tight band of energy twisting its way through her. She wasn't nervous at all; she felt calm, almost clinical, about what she was about to do. It wasn't that she had never picked up a man before. She had. But it had never been done in such a no-frills, deliberate manner. She had always approached her conquests softly, with smiles, flattery, indirect innuendo. Sometimes, depending on the type of man, she had even won them with disinterest. But the situation tonight would be different. She would need to be obvious but not crude. Blunt but not vulgar. The kind of man she needed would understand what she wanted. That she was not interested in anything more than a one-nighter. Yet he could not be the kind of man who pleasured women for a living. The kind of man who would hunt her down. Find out who she really was. Threaten her with blackmail. He would be the kind of man who would take what she gave him and then disappear into the heat of the Jamaican morning, never to bother her again.

Camille fingered the black lace teddy hanging from a padded pink hanger. It was a curvy little garment, which revealed almost as much as it concealed. It was deeply scooped in the back, with two conveniently placed red ties around the small of the back. The front of the frilly, lacy creation was designed to ride high on her bosom, giving away just the right amount of flesh without showing it all. A glimpse of dusky nipple would be possible through the mesh of the fabric, but only if she stood under direct light and, again, only if the material of the garment moved in just the right way. It was a tantalizing little number designed to draw male attention. And draw male attention she would. In her sexy little getup of mask, teddy, heels, and glitter, she was bound to be one of the hottest chicks there.

She dressed quickly now, sliding into the teddy, pulling the cups up and over her breasts. Reaching behind for the ties and handling those with quick, efficient fingers. She sat to cream her skin again. Shoulders. Elbows. Arms. Legs. An extra rub of lotion across the round of each heel. She directed a spray of perfume into the air and then stepped into the shower of fragrance, letting the droplets settle on her hair and skin. She sucked in a sweet breath and then sat to tend to her hair.

One of the requirements to get into the masquerade ball was that each partier dress in intimate apparel. Anyone who arrived in other dress would not be allowed in to mix with the other revelers. The thought of going to a party clothed in nothing but underwear had amused Camille at first, but she saw the benefit of it now. Relaxed dress meant relaxed inhibitions, which in turn meant that anything might happen.

She gave herself a pert little smile and reached for the black lace mask. Anything at all could happen tonight.

Harry Britton smiled at the scantily clad woman. "I'll have one of those," he said, reaching for a fluted glass of wine. "And another one for my friend."

The waitress, who was dressed like a half-naked

Bunny, with silk stockings, tight stomach, and over-flowing bosom, gave the two men standing before her an excited little laugh. She was well accustomed to serving all types of customers, but these two were simply two of the sexiest men she had seen in a long time. Her eyes flicked between them. It was hard to say which one was better looking. They were both about the same height. Same build. With hard, flat stomachs and long, long legs. But one had dark, brooding eyes with a headful of floppy black curls, while the other one had a close-cropped haircut, flirtatious coal black eyes, and very kissable lips. They were gorgeous. Simply gorgeous.

The girl smiled and offered the drinks. She could really go for either of them. But any fraternization between the guests and staff could get her fired. So, for now, she would just have to look and admire their tight, tight bodies. And cute little butts. . . .

Harry clapped Nicholas on the back. "Come on, man, this kind of party is just what you need. You're married, but you're not dead, right?"

Nicholas gave a hoarse chuckle. "I don't know why I let you talk me into coming here. Man, look at these girls." And he turned to look at a tall, long-legged woman who walked by clad in little more than a pink boa and matching heels. He shook his head.

"Jesus, Britton. If Mandy ever found out that I came here with you . . ."

Harry took a deep drink from his glass. "Mandy's

at home with Summer, the kids, and those girls. Who, by the way, are anything but innocent. That older one, Fancy or Francy or whatever her name is, had her foot right up my—"

He stopped in midsentence to say, "Lord have mercy. Look at that."

Nicholas turned and his lips curled. "Don't forget I'm a married man now, dog." But his eyes slitted in appreciation as a very tall, very sleek-looking woman with a curvy Coke bottle body walked by them in a mist of lace and expensive perfume.

Harry finished the remaining swallow of wine in his glass. "Now, *that's* my kind of woman. Look at those legs. Man. The things I'd like to do with that . . . Uhm." He followed the woman with his eyes. "You know I'm a leg man, right?"

Nicholas laughed. "I know you're a very sick man. What you need is a good decent woman. Someone to—"

Harry pressed his wineglass against Nicholas's chest. "Not tonight, man. Tonight and maybe tomorrow night, too, what I need is *that* kind of woman." He adjusted the fit of his black satin pajama bottoms. "Watch and learn."

Camille chose the middle stool at the corner bar. She sat carefully, draping one long leg over the other. She had been at the ball now for about an hour and had been very disappointed with the selection of men. Most of them were middle-aged and balding, with soft potbellies hanging over their much too tight shorts. Some were G-stringed, with awful hairy behinds; others were just awful, period. She had been considering returning to her suite when two fabulous-looking men had walked in. She'd noticed them immediately of course. And her heart sank a bit lower at the sight of them. She knew exactly what they were. And she had already made a firm decision against having anything at all to do with men like them. Sure, they were good-looking. Great looking if she was being totally honest. Their bodies were young. Hard. Hot. Their butts so tight and round it made tears come to her—

"I'll have some Dom."

The warm, husky voice cut through Camille's thoughts and she glanced at the man who had just settled himself on the stool right next to her. He was even more handsome up close. She sucked in a little breath. She had known that one of them would approach her. Men like them knew their trade well. They could always tell who was American and who had money. She pursed her lips in a quick little decisive movement. She would have to get rid of him firmly and quickly. She couldn't have him scaring away genuine prospects.

She opened her mouth to speak and then closed it again as he said in a very direct and puzzling fashion, "Hello."

She blinked at him for an instant. She had expected a different approach. An old, well-used line, perhaps. But not a simple, "Hello." And his accent was strange. It was cultured. An interesting blend of British and something else that she couldn't readily identify. If she wasn't absolutely sure that she was right in her initial assessment of him, she might even have pegged him as a member of the class of wealth she knew so well. But he was too young to have accumulated any appreciable sum of money, that she knew. Why, he could be no more than thirty-three or thirty-five. Of course, he might be one of those dot-com millionaires. But that was wishful thinking. What were the odds of running into someone like that at the first party she went to on the island?

Camille looked him over in a flickering glance. It would simply be too good to be true. And things that were too good to be true never ever happened.

She moved her leg away from his long warm thigh. He wasn't a dot-com millionaire; what he was, was a party boy who was probably hoping that she would pay for his drinks, among other things.

"How are you?" she said in a stiff little voice. She lifted her glass and took a delicate sip. Maybe he would get the message and just go away.

The man smiled at her and Camille felt a shiver of warmth puddle in her groin. God, but he had the blackest eyes she had ever seen. And those lips. They looked like the lips of a man who gave good—

"I'm sorry?" What was he saying to her? Didn't

he understand that she didn't want to talk to him? God, but he was persistent.

He extended a hand, and Camille realized that he was waiting for her to place her hand in his.

"Harry Britton," he said, and smiled at her again.

She gave him her cold palm, and the warmth of his flesh as it closed around hers caused a rash of gooseflesh to rise on Camille's arm. She tried to remove her hand with a little tug, but it remained locked in his grasp.

"Cold hands," he said, and Camille tilted her chin up. She knew exactly what he was going to say next. Men who said "cold hands" in that particular manner inevitably finished the statement with the tired and played-out, "Cold hands, must mean you've got a warm heart, huh?" And it always, always, made her sick.

She waited for him to complete his thought, but when he didn't, she asked in a clipped manner, "Can I have my hand back?"

Harry released the hand and then leaned both elbows on the curved lip of the bar. "You haven't told me your name, Miss . . . ?"

Camille shook her head. "Listen, Harvey—"

"Harry," he corrected in an extremely pleasant manner.

"Harry, then. You're wasting your time with me. Look around you. There are a lot of other women here. Why don't you go hit on one of them?"

Harry laughed. "A direct woman. I like that. So, I'm not your type then? My nose is too big for your tastes? Or maybe it's my butt?" And he got up for her to have a look.

Despite every effort to keep a straight face, a whisper of a smile tugged at the corners of her mouth.

"Ah, ah. I saw that," Harry said.

Camille tried to prevent her lips from curving into a smile. "Saw what?"

Harry sat again and leaned forward to say in a conspiratorial tone, "You know, I've been having this problem with women for ages now, and I just can't seem to figure it out."

"Figure what out?" The words were out before Camille remembered that she wasn't supposed to be talking to him.

Harry stroked the corner of his lower lip with a gritty thumb. "Well, women just don't seem to like me."

This time Camille laughed. He was good, this one. OK, she'd play along, for a little while. At least until the right man caught her attention.

"I really find that hard to believe, Mr. Harry Britton." She looked him over with shrewd eyes. "I'd be willing to bet good money that your success rate with women is pretty close to one hundred percent."

He placed a long index finger on her arm, and Camille looked down at it. It was so masculine.

Long and blunt, with a neat square-cut nail. And it felt so very good just resting there against her skin.

"So, I can't fool you then?"

She looked at him, eye to eye. He was a very handsome man. And, strangely, he had very kind eyes. If she hadn't decided against bedding a party-boy type, she would've chosen to spend the night with him. He was so interesting. And so damn sexy. Too damn sexy for his own good.

"I've been around a while," she said, "so I don't fool easy."

"Uhm," he said. "American?"

And Camille found herself agreeing with his guess before she could rethink the wisdom of doing so.

He nodded as though everything made complete sense and then asked, "Feel like dancing?"

Chapter Five

"But what about your friend?" Camille asked in a last-ditch attempt to forestall the inevitable.

Dancing with him had been a huge mistake; she realized that now. If she had had any sense at all, she would have stuck to her original plan and just sent him on his way. But that first dance had turned into a second and then a third, and before she knew it, she had been bumping and grinding with him like some adolescent caught in the throes of her first major crush. It had been like nothing else, the feel of his warm body pressed so tightly against hers. And she had pressed back against him, matching him exactly as he moved his waist in that rotating motion that Jamaicans called Wy-ning. She had been wild. Totally uninhibited. And he had laughed down at her, his eyes filled with fun, teasing her to go further and further still. And she had laughed back, moving a hand down to caress the smooth, muscular lines of his back, the round of his hard behind. She hadn't wanted to stop there. And it had seemed so very

right when he had bent his head to take her lips in a
warm kiss. She had almost lost track of things after
that. And only had the haziest of recollections of the
exact sequence of things after that first drugging
kiss. She had had another glass of wine, a handful
of spicy seafood appetizers, which Harry had fed to
her one by one. There had been more bumping and
grinding. A slow dance in a dark cozy corner. Then
the kissing had begun again. And each one had gone
straight to her head like a shot of vodka. But she had
given as good as she got, because she was just as tal-
ented as he was at this. And before she knew it, they
were in an elevator and she was mumbling her suite
number and pulling him back toward her. Anxious
for more. Always more. . . .

It was only when the smooth wood of the room
door pressed hard and cold against her back that she
remembered that Harry Britton was the wrong man.
He was wrong in every way. She couldn't sleep with
him. Instinct told her that somehow, someway, he
would be trouble. But he felt so very good. So very
right. What would it hurt to spend just a few hours?
Just a few hours. . . .

"You . . . you can't just abandon your friend like
that. You have to let him know. . . ." She made one
last half-hearted attempt.

"Nick can . . ." and Harry bent to gently nip at the
skin on the side of her neck, ". . . take care of himself."

"Shouldn't you tell him, though? Won't he . . .

won't he wonder where you've gotten to?" If Harry went for that one, her suite door would be firmly locked by the time he returned. She would be able to splash some water on her face. Cool herself down. And Mr. Smooth Harry Britton would not be the one spending the night between her sheets.

Harry laughed, a husky rumble that began somewhere deep within his chest.

"Nick Champagne? Worry where I've gotten to?" Harry put a hand between her legs and stroked in a manner that caused Camille's nails to curl into the skin of his arms.

"If you knew him the way I do," he said between delicious little circles of his thumb against the join between her legs, "you wouldn't spend a single," he pressed a butterfly kiss to the tip of her nose, ". . . solitary," another kiss to the left corner of her mouth, ". . . moment," a kiss to the right corner, ". . . worrying about him."

Harry brought a hand up to pull gently on the dusky round of a thrusting nipple, and a shudder of pure lust ran its way through Camille.

"Now. . . ." His breath touched her ear. "Where is your room key?"

Hot blood pounded its way beneath her skin, and she struggled for just a moment more with the voice of reason. She couldn't do it. She shouldn't do it. Not with him. *Not with him.* But . . .

He pulled her earlobe into his mouth. Sucked on it. Hard and sweet. His tongue darted into the whorls of her left ear, touching, tasting. Driving her crazy.

"The . . . the pouch at my waist." The words stammered out of her in short breathy gasps. It was too good. Too absolutely incredible. But it was just what she had needed if she was completely truthful. Just what she had needed. Because after this, what would she have? Lots of money and absolutely no sex. Life just wasn't fair. Why couldn't she have it all? Didn't some women manage to have it all? Her friend Lola did. She had bagged herself a hard, hunky husband who was spectacular in bed. Well . . . well, she deserved one last fling with someone like Harry Britton. Didn't she?

She bent her legs and allowed him to lift her as he shouldered the door open. Her head rested against the hard strength of his shoulder and she watched the play of light across his face as he carried her into the sunken sitting room, across the beautiful cream and mauve carpeting, and into the darkened bedroom.

"The first time," he said, placing her to rest gently against the chenille bedspread, "should be on a bed. The second and third times . . . ," he smiled down at her, ". . . you get to choose where."

Camille looked up at him dreamily. *What a man.* This was truly her fantasy. If she had planned the whole thing herself, she couldn't have done a better job. He was perfect, this Harry Britton. Perfect, at least, for what she needed tonight.

Harry bent forward to run his tongue along the deep cleft between her breasts, and Camille sucked in a sharp breath. Her heart pounded like a wild thing against her ribs, and she was tempted to grab him about the waist with her legs, wrestle him down to the bed, and have her way with him right then and there.

But, instead, she said in a voice that shook just a little, "Leave my mask on."

Harry propped an elbow on either side of her head and gave her an amused grin. "No name, now no face? A mystery woman, hmm?"

"That's right," Camille said, and she ran her hands across the splay of his shoulders, her fingers running into the little dips and thrusts of bone and sinew. He was a work of art, that was certain, and there was not a single ounce of fat on him anywhere. She was tempted to ask him what it was he did for a living. Had she been right about him? Was he really just a party boy? And how exactly did he manage to keep his body in such absolutely wonderful shape? But she withdrew the thoughts almost as soon as they occurred. She didn't want to know anything at all about him, and he couldn't know anything at all about her.

"Well, OK then, lady," Harry said, and he gave her a garland of kisses around the base of her neck. "I'll play tonight, but tomorrow I want to know all about . . . you."

Camille smiled and turned him slowly onto his

back. Tomorrow? Tomorrow she would be back aboard her private jet, pointed in the direction of the United States. And Harry Britton would never see her again.

Chapter Six

It was just past four o'clock in the morning, but Camille was still going strong. She had never been this insatiable before. Never been this absolutely uninhibited. And each time was better, more inventive, more incredible, than the last. She lay on her back now with the bedclothes in a tangle across the large four-poster, her legs parted and trembling with tension.

"Yes," she said, and her voice escaped in a sob of sound. "Sweet Jesus, yes. Right there. Right there."

Her fingers clasped Harry's head, pulling him closer to her as his tongue stroked slowly and with great thoroughness over and over her quivering nub of flesh. He nipped at the cloud of black hair with his teeth, pulling softly on several individual strands before slowly parting each brown fold and sucking delicately on its pink underside.

Unintelligible words bubbled from Camille's throat, and her voice became broken, harsh sound as she begged and then commanded him to enter her.

Harry took his time with her, holding her legs firmly with both hands, increasing the suction of his mouth and the stoking of his tongue as she scrabbled at his shoulders and tried to move him with force.

Tears pooled along the lower lids of her eyes and Camille began to sob and plead and cry. "Come on. You must. Now. You must."

Harry prolonged the delicious torture for just a moment more, and then he lifted himself, dragged her hips down closer, and entered her in one firm thrust.

Camille made a guttural sound of satisfaction at the good solid feel of him, and her neck arched involuntarily as he began to move. Slowly at first, so that she had to clamp her legs about his buttocks to urge him on. And then in a firm and thrusting rhythm that caused the bed to shudder and her voice to fill the confines of the suite. She responded to him like a wild thing, clawing at his shoulders, nipping at his skin, meeting him thrust for powerful thrust. She screamed his name, and he grunted in reply, holding her firmly and burying himself deep inside her, over and over and over again.

Harry stared down at her masked face through slitted black eyes. This was good. Maybe as good as it could get. *What a wild, wild woman.* It would be days, maybe weeks, before he'd had his fill of her. He had thought that she would be sufficient for just a one-night stand, but he hadn't expected her to be this . . . sweet. This demanding. *This incredible. . . .*

He drew her legs up around his neck and pulled her closer still. "You like that?" His voice was at once a question and a demand.

Camille responded to him in a whimper of breathless, gasping, moaning sound.

Harry buried himself within her harder, firmer, and his voice cracked with authority. "What's my name?"

She answered him in soft little gasps. And a hard smile twisted Harry's lips at the sound of her.

"And what's your name?"

Camille, in the throes of the sweetest release she had ever had, tossed her head back and gave him the answer he'd been after all night long.

Much later, to the wonderful sound of waves folding incessantly on the beach, they slept. Camille turned away from him with the flat of one hand resting against the exposed side of her mask, and Harry rested against the slim curve of her back, with an arm tucked snugly about her middle.

And for the first time in years Camille had sweet, peaceful dreams. She slept with her mouth half-open, her tongue pressed softly against her teeth. Harry slumbered without a sound, his body relaxed, satiated.

Camille opened her eyes just on the edge of dawn

as the sky filled slowly with soft pink light. Awareness came back to her in a mosaic of wonderful color, and a smile curved the corners of her lips. What a night. What an absolutely incredible night. It was definitely one for the record books. And one that she was sure to remember for the rest of her life.

She turned slightly to look at the man who still slept beside her. During the night, he had moved away from her. His fingers still rested on the dip of her waist, but Camille shifted these with ease and then lay still as he stirred for a second. Once he was again sleeping deeply, she rolled away from him and slid toward the edge of the bed. She was severely tempted to wake him and indulge in a repeat of what had passed mere hours before, but in the hard light of day, common sense prevailed. Harry Britton would ask way too many questions once he was awake and alert. Thank God she hadn't given him her name. At least she was reasonably sure that she hadn't given him her name. Things had gotten out of hand the night before. She had lost control, and she never ever did that. But who could blame her really? He had been so very, very good. Like no one she had ever had before.

Camille rested on the edge of the bed for a minute more and then quickly and quietly went about the business of dressing and packing her few items. She couldn't stay all weekend now as she had originally planned. Because if she did, she would have to bed Harry Britton again. And if she did that . . . well, God only knew what would happen if she did *that*. And she had worked much too long and much too hard to throw everything away for a good-time party boy, no matter how good in bed he was.

Packing everything away and neatly closing and zippering the bag took no more than five minutes. She had a quick look about the suite to make certain that she hadn't missed anything; then she removed the black lace mask, folded it neatly, and slipped it into her purse. She spent another minute hunting in the bottom of her roll-away bag for the little item she had brought for this very purpose. When she'd found it, she sat at the white lacquered vanity to write. The note was short and to the point. Camille placed her gift atop the paper and positioned it so that he was sure to see it before he left the suite. She had paid for the entire weekend, so she felt no guilt at all leaving him there fast asleep in bed. If her luck held, by the time he awoke, she would already be aboard the Learjet. He would be confused at first, maybe a little put out that she had abandoned him in such a manner. But her gift of diamonds would console him. Later, in years to come, he might remember her with fondness. She might even become a legend of sorts on the party-boy circuit. Harry would probably remember her as a freaky chick with whom he had spent an amazing few hours, once upon a Friday night, in the long, long ago. By then of course, she would be an old and very respectable married lady with two cocker spaniels and a large mansion in the Maryland countryside.

She got to her feet and stood for a moment more staring at the man who lay sleeping on the bed. A tinge of regret stole into her eyes. Money. Power. Extreme privilege. It would be enough. Wouldn't it?

She slung her purse across a shoulder, grabbed at the roll-away bag. It had to be enough.

At the door to the suite, she turned and whispered a very soft, "Good-bye, Harry." Then she was through the door and walking down the hallway. . . .

Chapter Seven

A beautiful salty breeze rolled in from the white-washed veranda, causing the drawn-back curtains to billow and crack. The soft sound of cloth on cloth brought the ripple of a frown to Harry's forehead. He stretched one arm and then the other and emerged from sleep in a slow, contented awakening of muscles and joints. Another stretch, this time of his long, lean back, and his eyes came open. Awareness returned quickly and he raised himself on an elbow and took a quick look about the bedroom. The unnatural stillness paired with the incessant flapping of the curtain brought him into a sitting position. The spot beside him was empty. Now, where the devil was the woman?

"Camille?" His voice was always a few shades deeper in the morning, and this morning it rasped around the edges in a manner that caused him to clear his throat and try again. He didn't give a damn about using her name. Sure, he had wrung it from her during the night, but that was neither here nor there as far as he was concerned. The night before had been a play, a wonderful, exotic, sexy farce played by two consenting adults. But the time for game playing was over as far as he was concerned, and he would know who and what she was. He hardly ever indulged in casual sex any longer, although he enjoyed giving that impression. For years, too many than he really cared to remember, he and Nick Champagne had been hard-living, smooth-talking playboys. Both lawyers. Wealthy. Never without a woman or two. But things were a bit different now. And the luster that such a lifestyle had once had, had dimmed somewhat. Oh, Harry wasn't ready for marriage or anything as confining as that anytime soon, but a steady relationship with a woman who could match him in bed and out of it? That was something he was definitely willing to try. And this woman, this Camille Roberts, might be just the one to hold his attention, for a while.

"Camille? Where are you?"

He swung a long leg over the side of the bed, flipped his discarded pajama bottoms toward him. She was obviously playing another one of her games. Hiding somewhere. Maybe she wanted him to find her, carry her back to bed, take her until she begged him for mercy. A grin sloped across his face. Well, if that was what she really wanted, he could certainly oblige her.

He slid into the pajama bottoms and went in search of her. The marble bathroom first. He yanked open the door and explored. He checked the deep Roman tub first and then the standing shower cubicle. He took a moment to splash some water on his face and emerged with a white terry towel about his neck. The game was beginning to pale just a bit. Where was the damn woman?

Harry wandered back into the bedroom and for the first time the possibility that she could have left him filtered into the back of his mind. He looked across at the vanity and his heart gave an uneven thud. A piece of paper. He hadn't noticed that before. He walked across, looked down at it, picked up the diamond-encrusted chain, and muttered, "What the hell is this?"

He read the note and then scrunched the paper in his palm. For a moment he stood motionless, his mouth tight, his eyes hard. Well. This was definitely a first. The hellcat had abandoned him with nothing more than a "Thank you so much for last night," *and* had had the nerve to *pay* him for his services with a gift of diamonds.

He folded the chain in on itself and bounced it in one hand. If this had happened to him ten years prior, he would have laughed it off, let the crazy woman go. But it meant something now. Who in blue blazes did she think she was? Leaving him a thank-you note. Paying him as though he were some cheap . . . His forehead wrinkled as another thought occurred to him. Jesus Christ. He laughed. Shook his head. She thought he was a gigolo. Now if that didn't just beat everything. *A gigolo.* He laughed again. Well, he would just have to go find the woman, return her little chain, and maybe fill her in on a couple of home truths. What kind of woman was she anyway? How could she behave in such a . . . a callous manner? Men did that kind of thing, not women. God in heaven, the way she had screamed, cried, and carried on the night before, she should have been kissing his feet this morning. As sweet as cherry pie. But instead of that, what did he get? The back of her hand, a thank-you note, and, to crown it all, *diamonds. Diamonds.* He glared at the chain in his hand. He had always thought that he possessed a pretty thick skin about most things, but this, this was something else entirely.

He walked across to the phone, picked it up, and dialed. When it was answered, he said in an abrupt manner, "Nora, I need a change of clothes. I'm at Hedonism in Runaway Bay. Suite Two A."

Camille passed most of the flight back to Dulles International on the phone. The plane had been ready and waiting for her at 7:30 a.m. sharp, just as she had requested. She had settled into the soft leather bucket seat, accepted a freshly squeezed glass of orange juice and a lightly toasted English muffin, and then allowed her mind to drift to Harry Britton for just a moment. She had promised herself on the way over to the private airstrip that she wouldn't think of him again. He was nothing to her. Nothing more than a good lay, as men often said about the women they bedded and then abandoned. But as she crunched on the muffin and washed away the smooth taste of premium light butter with little sips of orange juice, she allowed herself to think of him for just a bit. And as they lifted off and headed back across the blue Caribbean Sea, she felt his lips again, doing magical things that so many others had been unable or maybe unwilling to do. Saw his black and so sexy eyes, smiling at her in a manner that made her go all weak inside. Twenty minutes into the flight, she had had to fight against the desire to tell the pilot to turn the plane around. Camille was warm and wet and aching for something that only Harry Britton could give her. But she had been strong. Resolute. She had pulled out her telephone book and started making calls. Her wedding was only eight weeks away after all, and there was still a lot to do.

She dialed the wedding planner first and spent at least half an hour chatting animatedly about seating charts, guest lists, ice sculpture, white doves, fireworks, and cuisine. Then she called her fiancé, Anthony, and told him that she had decided to cut short her weekend getaway to Jamaica. He had been concerned at first, but she had managed to convince him that she hadn't suddenly come down with some dreaded illness, that she was perfectly fine. She had chatted with him for a few minutes more, feeling a strong twinge of guilt about her clandestine fling with Harry. But she had managed to keep these feelings nicely under wraps for the duration of their conversation, consoling herself with the thought that it wasn't her fault that she was a highly sexual woman.

She hung up the phone after about five minutes of chatter about nothing at all and stared out the little window at a beautiful patch of navy blue ocean, her mind churning. Was it her fault that Anthony had very little interest in sex? He was happy just managing his extensive portfolio of stocks and bonds, buying and selling commercial real estate, and puttering about in his garden tending to his roses. He didn't seem to understand that she was still a young woman with strong needs. Yes, he was fifty-seven years old, a good twenty-one years older than her almost-thirty-six years, but couldn't he at least try to give her what she needed? There were pharmaceutical products these days that worked quite effectively. She had tried talking to him about this once, and it was the only time that they had ever had a fight. He had become angry and defensive, and she had eventually dropped the matter. After all, he was very generous to her in other areas, and $50 million was a lot of money to give up just because of a little sex. She had decided then and there that she would just have to be strong once he put that ring on her finger. Because should she slip, should any trace of weakness creep in, she would be out there looking. . . .

Camille picked up the phone again with the

thought of that pressing in on her. If she should ever be weak when those urges took her, she would be out there looking for someone just like . . . Harry Britton.

She wet her lips, sighed. Why was life always this way? It gave one thing but took another. Why did young, virile men like Harry Britton never have two nickels to rub together? She couldn't marry a poor man. She was too . . . well, she was too used to the finer things of life. With Anthony's money, she could travel to Paris at the drop of a hat, if the urge took her. She could go shopping for the best jewelry at H. Winston's, just because. She could decide to buy a seaside condo anywhere in the world and spend the summer there just lazing about in the sun. . . . Now, what would a man like Harry Britton know about that kind of lifestyle? He had quite probably never even made it out of Jamaica. Just getting a chance to visit America would probably be the end-all and be-all of his little existence.

She sighed again and dialed. She couldn't ever marry a man like Harry. And because her own dear mama had damn near worked herself to death, and without a single ounce of appreciation being shown her by her employers, Camille had decided very early in her own life that she would not make the same mistakes. She would not be anyone's nine-to-five puppet. She would come and go as she pleased. Vacation for months on end, if it pleased her to do so. And, most important, she would not do a single stitch of work to live in such a manner. She would marry her money. And she was completely and totally unapologetic about her choice. She was not cut out for the corporate rat race thing. She wasn't like her friend Lola, who had made her money by scrapping and clawing her way to the top of the business world. Camille didn't want to prove that she was just as competent as any man. Hell, she already knew that. What she had always wanted, and this was the only thing that in her quieter moments brought her any sorrow at all, was children. Lots of them. Since she had grown up an only child, she had always dreamed of having a lively bunch of kids, running all over the house, tearing things up. And she would have been a good mother, too. A great mother. But it was not to be. It was not to be. She had made her choice now, and she would live with it. Her eyes misted as she put the phone to her ear and said, "Lola? Hey, girl, I'm coming back."

Lola St. James, who was at that very moment knee-deep in a particularly tricky corporate acquisition, put the file in her hand on the flat of her paperstrewn desk and asked in an amused manner, "So, did you find *the one*?"

Chapter Eight

Harry pushed open the oak-paneled door to his office suite, nodded a hello to his assistant, Nora Wilson, and then walked across to the little latticework station where his mail was always neatly sorted and waiting for him each day.

He gathered a pile of envelopes in one hand, went through them quickly, and almost without breaking his rhythm accepted a cup of black coffee with his free hand, bent his head, and took a long, steadying sip.

Nora Wilson watched him for a moment without comment. She had worked for Harry Britton for the past three years. Ever since he had settled permanently in Jamaica. And from the very beginning of her employment with his tiny law firm, she had been trying to think of a way to maneuver herself permanently into his life. She had researched his background with great care and had been deeply excited by what she had discovered. She had thought Harry Britton to be an up-and-coming lawyer with more looks and ambition than money or power. But she had discovered that there was much more to her boss than readily met the eye. For starters, she had discovered, after much digging, that he was the only son of the current Guyanese prime minister. Her palms had gone cold and damp at that bit of information. It was obvious to anyone with half a brain that the woman who married Harry would routinely rub shoulders with presidents, kings, sheikhs, and God only knew who else. She had also learned that he had a sister, who was now married to best-selling American author D. C. Lynch. And if that weren't enough, Harry was himself independently wealthy. Nora had not been able to find out how exactly he had made his money but knew that it had something to do with the Champagne family. A business alliance of some sort. Whatever it was, though, she didn't care. She had decided on her first day of employment that she would marry him. She knew he had no shortage of women friends and that he was certainly no celibate monk. But she felt sure that if she stuck with him through the love affairs and one-night stands, eventually he would wake up one day and notice her. Really notice her. Then. Then she would reel him in. And she didn't just want him for his money and influence, either. She liked him, too. He was a nice, easygoing kind of guy. In three years, she had never seen him in a bad mood. He was, as far as she was concerned, the ideal man. Handsome. Sexy. Brilliant. And—

"Did Clark Howard call?" Harry's voice made her blink rapidly and smile.

"No, sir. But you've got a visitor."

Harry stopped breathing for just an instant. A visitor. Well, damn it all, could the hellcat have returned? Tracked him down? He cleared his throat. "Who is it?"

Nora gave him her prettiest smile. "They asked me not to say, sir. I hope you don't mind?"

Harry drained the coffee cup and handed it back. "They?" And he softened the question with a comical lift of his eyebrows. "What are we talking here? Male or female?"

Nora wrinkled her nose and hoped he wouldn't be upset with her. "Why don't you go through to your office and find out?"

Harry shook his head in mock disbelief. "Nora Wilson. I don't know why I put up with you."

Nora grinned up at him and her heart did a tiny flip-flop in her chest at his answering smile. She knew exactly why it was he did put up with her. He just didn't know why he did, yet.

She opened her mouth to say something witty but was prevented from doing so by the opening of the inner office door.

"Harry Britton."

The voice made Harry turn and his face broke into an immediate smile. "Shorty. What are you doing here?" He beamed.

In response to his joking comment, the petite

woman standing in the doorway to his office propped her arms on her hips and said, "So, can't I just drop by to visit my baby brother if I feel like it?"

Harry walked across the short distance to sweep her up in a huge bear hug. He pressed a kiss to both of her cheeks, spun her around.

"Put me down, you great big idiot," Alana Collins said, batting at his shoulders.

Harry let her back down, pulled her into the inner office, and closed the door behind them. He hugged her again and Alana hugged him back tightly. She hadn't seen her big, beautiful brother in almost six months. Since he had moved away from Guyana, much to their parents' displeasure, she and Harry only saw each other now maybe once or twice a year. And for siblings who had always lived in each other's back pockets, that was not nearly often enough.

Harry stroked the side of her cheek. "You should've let me know you were coming, you crazy girl. Did Damian come with you? And the twins?"

His questions hit her in rapid-fire succession, and Alana gave him a suspicious little look.

"I came alone this time. You know, let Damian have some quality time with the twins. An eight-year-old boy and girl can be a handful . . . so he needs to know that." She tilted her head. "Are you OK, though?"

Harry chuckled. "Why shouldn't I be OK?" And

he changed conversational directions in a shot. "How are Mom and Dad?"

Alana plunked herself onto a long sofa facing a magnificent view of the ocean. "Mom and Dad are fine. Though they want you to come home." She played with a thread on the edge of her sleeve for a minute. "You know they've never accepted this whole thing about you living in Jamaica. They thought you were just going through a phase or something. Dad wants you back. You know . . . the old dream of you going into politics."

Harry came to sit beside his sister. "I know. I haven't completely ruled it out. I told him a couple years ago that I just needed some time."

Alana nodded and then said, "You know that woman out there is after you, right?"

Harry threw back his head and laughed. "What? Nora after me?" He pinched Alana's nose just as he used to when they were kids. "You think every woman is after me, you sweet girl."

Alana grinned. "Well, most of them are. But trust me on this one. Your secretary has the hots for you. All the signs are there. She was all bristly and defensive when I got here this morning. I guess she thought I was one of your girls. She only got nice and friendly when she realized who I was."

Harry gave her a considered, "Hmm," and Alana pushed him away from her with, "Don't 'hmm' at me. You'd better be careful. No playing around with her, if you know what I mean." She gave her brother a sudden sharp-eyed look. "Harry, you haven't already, have you?"

Harry gave her a wicked smile. "Played around with her, you mean?"

Alana slapped him on the hand and said, "I'm serious. I get really bad vibes from her. She might try to trap you into a situation or something. You know, a wealthy bachelor, with more money than sense."

Harry laughed at her description of him. "You just don't like her. That's the problem. It's a woman thing."

Alana pursed her lips. "OK. Don't say I didn't warn you. Anyway," she said, changing subjects, "I'm staying for a week."

"With the Champagnes?"

"No. I already spoke to Summer about it. I told her I was going to stay with you."

Harry gave her a surprised look. "With me? In my tiny place?"

"In your tiny place. There must be room for me somewhere. You'll just have to put your womanizing ways on hold for a few days."

"You mean I have to starve myself while you're here?" Harry teased.

"That's right." Alana smiled, and she gave him a loud kiss on one cheek. "That reminds me," and she fiddled in her pocket for a bit. "Summer gave me this for you."

Harry looked down at the crumpled newspaper clipping, his brow beginning to furrow. "What's this?"

Alana shrugged. "It's something about a wedding. Summer thought I knew about it. She said Gavin and Nicky wouldn't tell her anything about it."

Harry took the clipping and read it quickly. In the past week since his encounter with Camille Roberts, he had been pulling out all the stops to find her. He had been able to use his influence with the hotel manager to gather some basic information. He now knew her full name. The fact that she was an American and had arrived in the country aboard a private aircraft. He had even been able to discover her culinary likes and dislikes. But he had run right into a solid wall after that. The hotel manager had not been able to provide a home address for Camille, since she hadn't given one. What she had provided was the name of a dummy corporation, which had proven to be nothing more than another dead end.

Camille Roberts had covered her tracks well, and the fact that she had gone to such trouble to do so was something that intrigued Harry even more.

He had enlisted the help of a private detective, a very capable ex-policeman, who was even now checking the flight logs of each airport and private airstrip for any trace of a Camille Roberts.

"So? What's this all about?" Alana asked after a moment spent staring at her brother's face.

Harry read the snippet of words again, his heart beating in hard, heavy thumps. *Lola St. James is pleased to announce the marriage of Camille Roberts to financier Anthony Davis. The wedding and reception will be held at the St. James estate on Saturday, September 2, at two o'clock in the afternoon. . . .*

Alana pinched his arm and Harry finally gave her his attention. "It's probably nothing." He managed to smile even though he felt like someone had just sucker punched him. "Probably nothing at all."

Alana narrowed her eyes. She knew her brother well, and this was something, no matter what he had to say about it. "So, why do you look as though you've just discovered that you're adopted?"

Harry rewarded her with a laugh. His sister was as nosy as the day was long, and she would not stop digging until she had wormed every single bit of the sordid affair from him. She would pester him relentlessly. And she would quite probably begin to imagine that he had some sort of a romantic interest in the ridiculous woman. But it was no use, he would have to tell Alana. She would find out anyway.

"It's just this . . . ah. . . ." he cleared his throat, ". . . this woman."

Alana's eyebrows lifted a bit. A woman? The cause of his down-in-the-dumps expression was a woman? God be praised, this was a great piece of news indeed.

She tried to keep the smile she felt from showing and asked instead, "What woman?"

Harry shrugged. "Just someone I met recently." He looked down at the newspaper clipping again. "And here it says that someone with exactly her name is getting married. . . ."

Alana looked at the scrap of paper. Read it quickly. "Well, how do you know it's really her? Many people have the same name."

"I know," Harry agreed. "Nick has this news clipping service. You tell them what items you're interested in, and they search all of the papers for you. They must have run across this announcement in one of the U.S. papers."

Alana's heart pounded in her chest. "So, you've been looking for this . . . this person? This . . ." She looked at the piece of paper again. "This Camille what's her name?"

Harry stood and his gaze settled on the placid stretch of blue Caribbean Sea visible through the floor-to-ceiling plate-glass windows. If this person who was getting married was indeed the hellcat who had spent the night with him, it would certainly explain a lot.

His eyes followed a colorful little sailboat that bobbed peacefully somewhere out on the horizon. It would explain why she had gone to such trouble to cover her tracks. But why would she leave her fiancé behind in the first place? Fly all the way to Jamaica to have a night of wild sex with a complete stranger? And then fly out of the island the very next day? That made no sense. No sense at all. Unless—

"Harry? You're not listening to me."

Harry looked down at his sister. She was such a sweet person. And even though she badgered him constantly about getting married and settling down, there was no one he loved more.

He grinned at her. He could tell by the look in her eyes that she had come up with some scheme or another. "What? I didn't hear you."

"I know you didn't hear me," Alana agreed in an exasperated manner. "What's the matter with you anyway? One minute you look as though you've lost your best friend, and the next you're staring at the ocean and saying some nonsense about covering tracks and sailboats. Harry dear," and she got up to put her arms about his waist, "you're just going to have to go and find this Camille person." She gave him a little shake. "Right?"

Twin pairs of black eyes met. "And if it turns out that she is the woman in the paper who's getting married?"

Alana shrugged, and for a moment she looked exactly like her brother. "If you really want her, then you stop the marriage. You break it up."

Chapter Nine

"Girl, look at this." Lola St. James turned to show Camille the silky slip of fabric hanging from one of the padded hangers on the lingerie rack. "Now, you can't tell me that this won't turn him on."

"Look at what?" Camille bellowed over the pink and white dressing room door.

Lola removed the wispy red garment and handed it over the top of the door. "Any man with even an ounce of life left in him has got to want to just throw you down and tear every inch of this off with his teeth."

Camille chuckled. "You're so crazy. You know Anthony doesn't want anything to do with me in that department. It's a dead issue. Believe me. Anyway, I'm here to get a wedding dress, remember? And this one. . . ." She grunted as the pull of fabric tightened around her rib cage. "This one is too tight."

Lola pushed through another rack of designer gowns, stopping to finger an old-fashioned high-necked dress with a line of pearl buttons running down the back. Lola lifted the dress out and looked it over. "You're a size six, aren't you?" And at Camille's grunt, Lola opened the door and handed the dress through with, "Try this."

Camille stepped out of the swirl of fabric and plopped herself onto a padded stool. "God. I hate this. I've tried on at least a million of these dresses and none of them look good."

Lola pulled another one out and held it up to the light. "Don't complain to me," she said. "I told you months ago to have the dress custom-made. But you wanted to do it your way. Now six weeks before the wedding, you still don't have a dress. And let me tell you, this designer warehouse is not the best place to look when you're in a hurry for anything."

"I know. I know," Camille agreed, and she wiggled herself into the new gown and sucked in her stomach. "But I have to pay for this . . . this dress myself. I can't use his money, for God's sake. And you know how expensive—"

"Don't even start with me and that," Lola said, cutting her off. "You know what I think about that whole thing. You should have more than enough to spend on your own wedding dress. You should own at least one company by now. But what are you doing? Running about the world spending other people's money."

Camille's head popped around the lip of the door. "I can't believe you just said that."

Lola folded her arms. "Why shouldn't I say it? Isn't it true?"

Camille's mouth worked soundlessly for a second. "Well, not everybody can be like you. Waking up at the crack of dawn. Working until midnight many days. Buying and selling companies. Making millions of dollars. I just don't want that kind of life."

Lola made a sound of disapproval, and Camille said, "I really don't."

"Well, what kind of life do you want? Don't you want to do something useful? Make a difference in the world?"

Camille swooshed out in the new gown. "I don't want to make the kind of difference you want to make. I just want . . ." She turned her back for Lola to fasten the scores of tiny buttons running down the back of the dress. "A home and family. That's what I want."

"You're just plain old-fashioned crazy," Lola shot back as her fingers fastened and smoothed the ruffles of fabric. "You want a home and family, so who are you marrying? A man who probably doesn't want that kind of a home, and who definitely doesn't want any kind of family." She finished the last button and said, "Turn around."

"You just don't understand," Camille sighed. "You know I'm getting older. I'll be thirty-six in September. I can't just wait around forever for the right man. You know that once you hit forty, they say it's easier to be killed in a terrorist incident than it is to find a man who'll marry you."

Lola held up a hand. "I don't believe in all that. What you really need is a good man. One who won't put up with your—" The ringing of her cell phone caused Lola to say, "Wait a minute. I have to get this. It might be important."

Camille looked at herself in the wall of mirrors and listened to her friend with one ear. Lola was really a great chick and most of the time she was right about things, but this time she didn't have a clue. Just because Camille didn't want to have to work for a living, did that make her a bum? A wastrel? Just a few generations ago, most women were homemakers anyway. So why was it so bad if that was all she wanted to be? Why did she have to be some corporate type with black patent-leather pumps, silk stockings, and a power suit? Why couldn't she just take it easy? Cook for her family. Keep a cozy home. Tend to the gardens. Go shopping from time to time. Why couldn't she? She came from generations of hardworking women who had done a lot of work but gotten very little to show for their labor. Her mother had been a seamstress. A hardworking woman who toiled from sunup to sundown. But when she had passed, she had had a sum total of two thousand dollars to her name. Two thousand dollars. After an entire lifetime of work. It was shameful; that's what it was. Just shameful.

"Well," Lola said, and she closed her flip phone with a little snap. "That was an interesting call."

Camille pulled at the skirt of the gown and asked in a distracted manner, "The acquisition's going to go through?"

Lola beamed at her. "Of course that's going to go through. But I wasn't talking about that. Does the name . . . Champagne mean anything to you?"

Camille frowned at herself in the mirror. The dress was just terrible. The sleeves were too big, the neck so high she felt as though she were choking, and the lacy ballroom-style skirt was just plain ridiculous. She turned to look at herself over the round of a shoulder and asked in a slightly irritated manner, "What? Champagne? What do you mean, does Champagne mean anything to me? I've already arranged for several cases of the best French Champagne to be delivered—"

"Not that Champagne," Lola cut her off. "Nick Champagne."

Camille stopped fiddling with the dress and gave her friend a genuinely blank stare. "What?"

Lola pulled her away from the mirror and sat her down. "Nicholas Champagne. Does that name ring a bell?"

Camille shrugged. "No. Should it?"

Lola sat beside her. "Never heard of the Champagnes, huh? Champagne Shipping? Champagne Global Financial Services? The Champagne Building in D.C.? No? Well," and she gave Camille a huge gamine grin, "that's great. Just peachy."

Camille stood in a rustle of silk and lace. "You're working too hard. What do I care about Champagne Fishing or some building in D.C.? I'm trying to buy a wedding dress here, so girl, try to focus. Don't forget I'm getting married in six weeks. Now," she said, spreading her arms wide, "what do you think of this one?"

Later that evening, with the heat of the day still hanging over the D.C. metro area, Camille packed her shopping bags into the back of her powder blue BMW roadster and headed deep into the heart of suburban Maryland. She had spent more than four hours hunting for a wedding gown, and she still could not say that she had found the perfect one. She was vaguely annoyed by the entire process. Why didn't anyone have exactly what she wanted? There were hundreds, thousands, of dresses, but they were all wrong in some little way. It was either one thing or the other. Too much lace. Not enough satin. Good pearls, but in the wrong place. An A-line skirt when it should be full. Sleeveless when sleeves would have made the dress perfect. And then Lola, who was always so practical and levelheaded about everything, had gone completely off the beam. She had made Camille try on one ridiculous dress after another, all the while carrying on and on about Champagnes, fate, true love, and all sorts of other nonsense. She knew exactly what Lola was up to, of course. She had been against Camille's marrying Anthony Davis from the very beginning, and now that the wedding was just around the corner, Lola was trying her best to sabotage the entire thing. But her little scheme wouldn't work. Camille was completely determined to marry. And nothing, save the intervention of God, would stop her from becoming Mrs. Anthony Davis on the afternoon of Saturday, September 2.

Camille drove into the setting sun with the thought of that beating a tattoo in her head. She was going to be happy. Her marriage was going to work out. And not only that, she was going to have that passionate relationship with Anthony that she needed. She had been thinking about what Lola had said about true love and the importance of going after and getting what was yours. And Camille had come to a firm decision about things. No longer would she accept chaste little kisses. Or the occasional hug and pat on the behind from Anthony. She was going to put it to him without delicacy or preamble. She was a highly sexed woman, and if he wanted to keep her happy, then he would have to keep her happy. She was more than willing to provide whatever props he might need. At Lola's insistence, she had bought several more items of slinky bed wear. Meshy little peekaboo garments that were designed to get a man's blood pumping. And pumping she would have him that very night. As soon as she arrived at the estate house. She'd take a quick shower. Turn some music down low. Dim the lights. And then let nature and a little lace take their course.

She swept a curl of hair away from her face, pushed her sunglasses higher up on her nose as the tension left her. It was a wonderful evening. The day had burnt itself to a mellow orange-gold, and a soft wind pulled at the edges of the silk scarf she had wrapped stylishly about her head. She reached a hand to turn up the radio as the warm and vibrant voice of Oleta Adams drifted from the speakers, singing beautifully about the rhythm of life.

Camille sang along with Oleta, tapping her fingers against the steering wheel and bobbing her head in time. There was an inscrutable rhythm to life. There was no question about that. Life. Death. Joy. Sorrow. Everything was connected. Everything in sync. And life would make sense sooner or later. She had to believe that. No matter how clouded, how unclear, things might seem now.

Her brow rippled in thought. Her life wasn't so very terrible. And she wasn't such a bad person, either. Sure, she had flaws, but that just meant she was human. She had her good points, too. Just like any other normal person. Some might think she was a gold digger, but she wasn't. Not really. Well, OK, maybe she was. But she had a good heart. And she would make Anthony a good wife. She wouldn't cheat on him. No matter how bootylicious the man.

No matter how much like Harry Britton he might look.

Camille frowned at the passing countryside. She had promised herself that she wouldn't think of him again. There was absolutely nothing to be gained from thinking of him. Harry was just a wonderful sexy little memory. Nothing more. Nothing less. And she just had to prevent him from popping into her head without warning like that.

She turned into the Princeville estates section and forced herself to focus on the beauty of the rolling green lawns and the shimmering little lakes. Anthony's house was the largest in the development, surrounded by a tall black wrought-iron fence and a cluster of shrubbery. It was a nice house, although it lacked a certain feminine something. But that was all right; after they were married, she would soften up the place with rugs and elegant curtains and lots of other little touches that men somehow never seemed to think about.

She swept up the cobblestone drive, punched in the code for the gate, drove into the courtyard, and parked right next to his Mercedes-Benz S500 sedan. She walked around to the trunk to unload her bags and wondered if she should toot the horn to let him know she had arrived. She had told him that she would come over at around eight thirty. And she was a full hour and a half early.

Camille glanced at her watch, slammed the trunk shut, and bent for her bags. It would be a nice sur-

prise for him. She was hardly ever early for anything. In fact, she was more often than not late for
everything. Sometimes very late.

Her heels made a clicking sound on the smooth
stones, and she stopped for a minute to admire a
cluster of blood-red roses growing from a bush at
the front door. She stroked the soft face of a flower
and then, on impulse, pulled the head off and stuck
it behind an ear. She let herself in, shuffled her
shoes off at the door, and then padded on bare feet
to the living room. The house was largely in darkness, so she rested her bags on a table and spent a
few minutes turning on lights. She looked about the
room once she was finished. Anthony did have good
taste. She had to give him that. The cream and black
decor was nice. A bit too masculine for her tastes,
but nice nevertheless. Of course she would change
things little by little once they were married. Vases.
Flowers. Throw cushions. Then eventually the entire
color scheme. She had a grand plan for the entire
house. It was going to be beautiful by the time she
was finished with it. And she would consult him,
too, about his likes and dislikes. She just wasn't going to force all the changes down his throat. She was
going to be a good wife to him. And maybe in time,
with a little bit of coaxing, he might even agree to
have . . . one child? She could be satisfied with just
one. Boy or girl. It didn't matter. And she'd be very
careful not to spoil the child. There was always a
tendency to want to spoil children who didn't have

any siblings. But she wouldn't do that. She would raise a well-balanced, healthy child. And they would be happy in their little family. Happy and content. And very soon, maybe in just a year or two, she wouldn't even remember Harry Britton. Not his eyes. Not his lips. Not his scent. Not anything at all.

The squeak of a floorboard in the master bedroom directly above the staircase caused her to look up and smile. So, that's where Anthony was. She had thought that she might be able to sneak into the master suite, take a quick shower, and then, all decked out in red high heels and short silky lingerie, surprise him in the study. But maybe what she'd do instead, since he was already in the bedroom, was a titillating striptease number. Men always loved that. A little shimmy, a little shake. A glimpse of bosom, a wiggle of butt. He'd be hot for her then. Or as hot as he could get.

Camille stopped outside the bedroom door and looked down at the bags in her hands. Anthony never seemed to mind how much money she spent. In fact, he always encouraged her to spend more. So she wasn't bothered about him complaining about her shopping spree. He had given her a credit card a month after proposing marriage and had said with a smile, "Have fun with it. Buy whatever you want. Just let me know if you get anything really big."

Her lips curled. He was a generous man. A very generous man. And she was lucky to have him. There were no perfect situations in life after all, and life with Anthony would be better than it would be with most men half his age.

She opened the door quietly and slipped in. She put her bags in a little floor-to-ceiling oak wood closet standing by the door and then called in a soft voice, "Honey?" The room was in darkness, too, and it took her a few minutes to get accustomed to the lack of light. When she could see clearly, she laughed. The little sitting room was in total disarray. There were shirts and trousers, socks, and several pairs of shoes scattered all over the floor.

Camille went about the room quickly, picking up things, folding and placing them on the arm of a sofa. She smiled to herself. Well, he had been in a big hurry to get into bed. At least now she knew he wasn't perfect. She had always marveled at the fact that he was such a very neat and tidy person. Strangely, this disorder pleased her. Made her feel hopeful. She could live very satisfactorily with a man who wasn't absolutely organized all the time.

When she was through, she stacked all of the clothes together on the chair and arranged the shoes in the closet. There. Now that would show him, if he had any doubts at all about it, that she was good, solid wife material.

A little sound brought her out of the closet. It was a soft bleating little noise that made worry wing its way through her. That was Anthony's voice. Definitely Anthony's voice. Oh no. Why hadn't it occurred to her? Was he sick? He was sick. That explained why the entire house had been in darkness. Why everywhere was in a mess. He was lying in bed as sick as a dog, and here she was messing about with clothes. Her nostrils flared, and her hands went cold as the thought struck her. Maybe it was a heart attack. Jesus. He was having a heart attack and was calling out for help. Maybe he was dying.

She was at the door to the inner suite in half a beat.

"Anthony?"

Camille flung back the door, and the trickle of sound that left her lips became a strangled, "Oh my God. Oh my God. Oh my God."

Chapter Ten

"Harry." Alana shifted a few more items around in the tight little cupboard and bellowed again. "Harry. It's not here."

Harry emerged from the bedroom, phone tucked beneath his chin.

"Just a minute, Nick," he said, and he placed the portable phone on a table and walked into the small utility kitchen.

"You know," he teased, "for such a little thing, you really have a loud voice."

Alana gave him a speaking look and said, "Oh, shut up. Where's the picnic basket? I've searched all the cupboards above and below. You are *such* a slob. Do you even know where anything is in this place?"

Harry shrugged in a good-natured manner. "You just don't understand my system, Dr. Collins. OK. Plates, cups, knives, and forks. You know the things I use every day?"

Alana gave him an unimpressed, "Uhm-hmm."

"Those I keep right here." He pulled open a cupboard door beneath the sink and pointed to the stash inside.

"So, you just throw everything together, huh? Knives, forks, spoons, pots, just everything."

"And," Harry continued, completely unfazed by her tone of voice, "that picnic basket you were hollering about." He scratched the side of his head. "That should be . . . right here. No. Wait a second; I did some laundry last week. So . . . that means . . . it should be in the bedroom closet. I think I put some laundry in it last week."

Alana shook her head. "God. You really need someone to look after you. Why don't you hire a housekeeper or get yourself a—" Her mouth snapped closed on the word. She had very nearly said "wife." But Alana knew that if she kept harping on and on about why he should settle down and get himself married, he might never do it at all. His strong interest, though, in this Camille Roberts person was very promising. Very promising indeed. But Alana wouldn't push. She would just stand back and let things happen naturally. This woman might be just the one to cool him down a bit. Tame him by just a little. She would have to be a special woman, though. A very special woman.

Harry bent forward to kiss his sister on the cheek, but Alana pulled away with, "Don't you try to suck up to me now. A grown man living like this. You should be ashamed."

He grinned at her and went back to his phone

call. He passed the next hour sprawled flat on his back in the middle of the king-size bed in his room, talking over strategy with Nicholas Champagne. They had both spoken to Lola St. James. Nicholas had called her first and then Harry had called and spoken to her later in the evening of the same day. They had decided to do things this way since the Champagne name was well-known in the United States and, given Lola St. James's stature in the business community, she was more likely to be willing to talk to a Nicholas Champagne than to a Harry Britton. And, surprisingly enough, she had seemed happy to hear from him. They had spoken for about half an hour, and he had gotten a very good feel for the lay of the land. Camille Roberts was a high-society girl. A gold digger who would marry anyone at all just so long as he had some money. She was currently engaged to marry a much older man who, for whatever reason, could not cut the mustard in bed. Hence her impromptu trip to Jamaica and her subsequent hasty departure.

Harry had listened to the entire pathetic story with a growing sense of relief. Thank God the hell-cat had mistaken him for a good-time guy. If she had only known that the man she had so casually abandoned after a night of wild sex was an even better catch than her older fiancé, Harry might have found himself in a hell of a situation. Women like Camille Roberts left him cold. Made him know with a great degree of certainty that his decision to remain a bachelor for as long as he possibly could was the right one. He had been on the verge of hanging up the phone and putting the damn woman out of his mind for good when Lola St. James had stunned him with an audacious suggestion. A proposal, of sorts. She wanted him to romance Camille away from her fiancé, Lola said. She would fly Harry to the U.S. aboard her private plane and would put him up in a modest apartment while he carried out the job. She would pay him well for his trouble, too. High five figures. And for just one month of work.

Harry had been so taken aback by the very calm and blunt manner in which she had set forth her plan that for a few seconds he had actually been robbed of speech. Then the humor of the situation had taken ahold of him, and he had begun to laugh. Before he had been told all of the sordid details of Camille Roberts's life, he had intended to seek her out. Fly to America. Do whatever it took to convince her that she should put her upcoming wedding on hold. But all of these plans had gone right out the window once he had realized exactly what kind of woman she really was. And now for her friend Lola to make such a proposition . . . It was almost beyond belief.

Lola had laughed along with him, her voice warm and guttural. Harry had finally said, "Good God in heaven. I'm having just about the worst month of my life."

It had taken some amount of explaining, but he told her in as nice a manner as he could manage. He

was to-the-point without giving away too many details. He could not possibly take her up on her offer,
since he was, contrary to popular thought, in fact
quite a wealthy man himself. He hung up quickly
after that, since he'd had a strong suspicion that
Lola had been about to suggest another scheme of
some sort.

He called Lola back the next day, though, with a
proposition of his own. He had spent almost half the
night thinking about it. And, he told her, if she agreed
to provide him with the necessary support and, of
course, if Camille's marriage was somehow no longer
in the cards, he would cure Camille Roberts once and
for all of her gold-digging ways. Women like Camille,
in his opinion, were in need of the kind of therapy that
only a man like him could administer. And in later
years, once she had finally found a man who would
marry her, she would thank Harry for his tutelage.

Harry had thought that he might have to convince
Lola to take part in his little plan, but to his surprise
she had jumped at his suggestion and assured him
that Camille's marriage was not a problem. Lola
would take care of it.

Harry rolled into a sitting position now, in the
middle of the bed, and spoke into the phone. "What
about Summer, though? Will she help out?"

On the other end of the line, Nicholas gave a
laughing response. "Summer? She loves nothing
better than this sort of stuff. She'll help. And she'll
get Gavin and Mandy to do the same."

"Good," Harry said. "I'll see you in a bit then. By the way, is it too much to hope that Summer's cousins won't be at this thing?"

Two hours later, Harry, now freshly showered and dressed in a ragged pair of cutoff jeans and a faded blue T-shirt, climbed into his dark green Range Rover. He turned the engine on and then leaned on the horn.

"Lani. Come on. We're late."

Alana appeared at the apartment door and gave him an irritated wave. She was on the phone again and Harry shook his head. She was no doubt talking to her husband yet again. God in heaven. The man hardly gave her enough room to breathe. He had already called her three times for the day, and it wasn't yet two o'clock in the afternoon.

Harry wound down the window and let a cool billow of ocean breeze fill the car. Not even if he did marry at some point in the distant future would he ever let any woman have him so completely whipped. Her husband, Damian, was a nice enough guy, of course. Granted, Harry hadn't liked him very much in the beginning, but over the years he had grown to respect and even admire Damian. But Harry's sister had the poor guy so trained that if she said, "Jump," his response would be, "Yes, dear." It made Harry cringe to think that a grown man could be so soft. His sister was a lovable cuddly little thing, but Jesus, a man had to be strong about certain things.

Harry leaned on the horn again, and after a moment, Alana came trotting down the stairs with the wicker hamper slung across her arm. She pulled open the passenger side door, got in, and slammed it behind her. "Lord have mercy, but you're an impatient old cuss. I was talking to Damian."

Harry put the car in gear and gave her a bland, "So, what's new?"

Alana reached across and pinched him on the arm. "Just you wait until you get married. Then you'll know what I'm talking about."

Harry nosed the Rover into the tight Ocho Rios traffic before saying, "Are we talking about Harry Britton? Or some other poor fool?"

Alana chuckled. "Well, we'll see, Mr. Harry Britton. We'll see."

Harry let the comment go and asked instead, "So, how are the twins getting on without you? Behaving themselves?"

Alana wound down her window and let the wind pick at her corkscrew curls. "Melly's a very independent little girl. As long as she has her books to read, she won't give any trouble at all. Harold, your namesake, is another matter entirely. Damian's going on a book tour as soon as I get back, and he's thinking about taking little Harold along. I think it's a mistake, but . . ." She spread her fingers.

Harry turned onto the coast road and headed up the hill toward Champagne Cove. "Little Harry'll be OK. He's not such a bad little kid. And believe me, I know. At his age, I was a holy terror. Some of the things I got up to . . ."

Alana laughed. "Don't remind me." And then she lowered the window all the way and yelled, "Hey, Amanda. Amanda Champagne."

Harry slowed the Rover beside the jogging woman. "What are you doing out here? Hasn't the picnic started?"

Amanda jogged on the spot, breathing evenly. "I'm not going."

Harry and Alana exchanged a lightning glance.

Harry nudged Amanda on the arm in a playful manner. "What do you mean, you're not going? It's a big family thing. You have to go."

Amanda gave Harry a hard-eyed look. "I don't have to do anything at all. I'll see you later. Alana, I'll call you." And Amanda took off running again.

Harry pursed his lips in a silent whistle. "Nick's gotta handle that before it gets out of hand."

Alana turned to look behind her, and she stared at Amanda's retreating figure until the belly of the hill blocked her from view.

"Wow," Alana said after a stretch of silence. "I've never seen her like that before. What's going on between her and Nicky?"

Harry shrugged. It wasn't for him to say. He'd al-

ready given Nicholas his two cents on the matter.
What more could he do?

Alana chewed on the side of her lip for a moment
and then blurted out, "Did you notice . . . She
seemed to be mad at you, Harry. Did you and
Nick . . . ? Oh my God." She covered her mouth
with a hand. "Harry, you didn't."

Harry turned in his seat to give his sister a genuine look of bewilderment. "Didn't what?"

"Have you and Nick been . . . been carousing like
you used to before he got married? Going to all of
those nasty little places and picking up all kinds of
loose women?"

Harry swallowed and turned his attention back to
the road. She was uncomfortably close to the truth.
But he and Nick had only gone to Hedonism once.
And Nick had left the masquerade ball long before . . . or just around the time that Harry and
Camille had left the party. And Nick had been alone.
Could Amanda have found out that Harry was re-
sponsible for Nick being there? He had been foolish
to talk Nick into accompanying him there. Now,
maybe because of this momentary slip, he had
helped make things even worse between Nick and
Amanda.

Harry scratched the back of his neck, and Alana
gave him a tight-lipped look.

"What is it? Is Nick cheating on her?"

Harry cleared his throat. He couldn't say for sure

whether Nick was or not. But if Harry had to guess, and his guesses were usually pretty good, he would say that Nick wasn't cheating on his wife. At least not yet. But if Amanda continued to give her husband the cold shoulder, then who could say what might happen?

"Nick isn't cheating. At least I don't think he is."

Alana made a little disbelieving sound. "So, why is she mad at you?"

"I don't know, Lani. Nick and Amanda are having some marital problems, and whatever they are, I really don't think we should interfere. Let them work things out for themselves." There was the slightest trace of irritation in his voice, and Alana gave him a look of surprise.

"You're angry with me?"

Harry ruffled her hair with a big hand. "You know I'm not. I'm angry with myself. And don't ask me what I mean, because I'm not going to tell you."

Alana clicked her tongue and shifted toward the window as the Rover turned into Champagne Cove and headed down the drive toward the beach. She was silent for such a long stretch that Harry nodded to himself and muttered, "Right. Here we go." By the stiff way in which she was holding her head he knew without question that she was going to give him hell later.

He stopped the SUV under a stunted mango tree and cut the engine. The sounds of laughter, music, and children's voices drifted up from the beach.

Harry hopped out. "Leave the basket. I'll get it," he said when his sister attempted to lift it out. He came around, grabbed it, and asked, "What's in here anyway?"

Alana, whose brief moments of upset never lasted very long, slapped Harry's hand as he attempted to find out for himself what was in the hamper.

"Leave that alone," she admonished. "It's Guyanese cheese sandwiches and some chicken curry."

Harry patted his stomach. "Couldn't have come at a better time. Come on." And they stepped over a few tiny rocks and then walked down the wooden ramp leading to the beach.

A strong breeze blew Alana's hair into a wild mess, and she lifted a hand to scrape a few strands back behind her ears.

Harry sucked in a deep breath. "Don't you just love all this? The sand, the ocean, the family?"

Alana gave him a secretive little smile and waved at Summer, who was knee-deep in a breaking wave with Adam held high before her, squealing in delight.

"We're finally here," Alana cupped her hands against the wind and shouted as loudly as she could.

Summer waved and beckoned them over. "Go ahead," Harry said. "I'm going to get myself a burger. And . . ." He shaded his eyes against the sun. "Hang around with the guys." He lifted a hand to call out, "Yo, Mik. Rob. . . ."

• • •

On the other side of the ocean, holed up in a very comfortable suite on the St. James estate, Camille was doing some calling out of her own. She sat in the middle of a rumpled four-poster, with blanket and sheet askew and hair in complete disarray.

"That . . . that bastard," she said again. "And to think, to think that I never suspected. But I should've known. I really should've known. Him not wanting to touch me until we were married. It was a dead giveaway. I hear all of this stuff all the time about these DL brothas. But I just didn't think it could happen to me. *Me*. God. I'm such a fool."

Lola perched on the edge of the bed and asked in a very calm manner, "So, what does this mean? Is the wedding off?"

Camille gave her a slack-jawed stare. "Is the wedding off? Are you completely crazy? Of course the wedding's off. Do you think I'd marry a man like that? I caught him in the act, I'm telling you. In the very act." She wiped the edge of an eye with the sleeve of her bathrobe. "And he actually had the . . . the *nerve* to come after me with . . . with everything hanging down like an old burro. Telling me that nothing had changed. That we could work things out. I could still have *the life* . . ." She laughed in a harsh manner. "Work things out. Can you believe it? Jesus." She covered her mouth and began to cry. "Oh, God in heaven, what am I going to do? I don't have a job. I've got some money saved, but not enough to last me more than maybe a few months. I was really banking on this marriage, you know? What am I going to do now?"

Lola wrapped an arm about her. "It's not so bad," she said, and she pulled Camille into a tight hug. "You might have found out all of this after you were married. And how much worse would that have been for you? Besides, you don't have to worry about a place to stay. . . . You can stay right here with Chaz, Jamie, and me for as long as you like. There's plenty of space."

Camille sobbed even harder. "I'll be thirty-six in September," she managed after a bit, "almost forty. And I've got nothing. Nothing to show for it. I've made a mess of things. You were right all along. About everything."

"Come on, Cam," and Lola patted her on the back. "Thirty-six isn't nearly old these days. You can still do anything at all you want with your life. Anything."

"But I don't have any skills," Camille croaked.

"What do you mean, you don't have any skills? You've got good people skills. Maybe you can turn that into something. You know, maybe go into PR or something like that. I can pull some strings. . . . Lots of people owe me."

Camille looked up at her, eyes red and brimming. "I am kinda good with people, huh?"

Lola nodded. "Good with people but dumb with men."

Camille blew her nose in a napkin. "Don't go saying, 'I told you so,' now."

Lola spread her fingers in an expressive gesture. "I'm not going to say anything. But just remember . . . in the future, if you come across anything that walks like a duck . . . you know what I mean?"

Camille nodded. She had been all kinds of a fool. She should have known that Anthony didn't like women. All of the signs were there, if she had only had the eyes to see them. But she had been so excited about finally finding the sort of man she had always wanted. One who was wealthy enough and generous enough to keep her in the kind of style she deserved. Now she'd be forced to live exactly the kind of life she didn't want to live. Scrambling up in the mornings at the crack of dawn, hustling down some food at the speed of indigestion, and then pelting out into the rush-hour traffic to do a job she really didn't want to do. It was just too bad. And it wasn't like her to pin all of her hopes on one thing, either. But she had been so sure about Anthony. He'd been good to her.

She sniffed in a pitiful manner and flopped back against the soft pillows. Maybe there was something else she could do other than go out looking for a job. She still looked good. Damn good, actually. Why couldn't she find another rich man to marry? There were lots of them around, after all. There were Wall Street men, sports stars, musicians, actors. But time was ticking along. In just four years they'd all think she was some pathetic old broad. Besides, most of these rich guys were married before they were thirty-five. So, at best, if she managed to find one, she was going to be five, maybe ten years older than he was. Anthony be damned. Look at what he had done to her.

Camille shuffled down farther in the bed and pulled the blankets up. Everything was so confusing. It was almost like she couldn't think straight at all. What she really needed was a good long vacation. Somewhere on the ocean. Somewhere she could get her head together.

"Here's Annie with some lunch for you." Lola smiled at her housekeeper as she came forward with a tray of cups and plates.

Camille turned onto her side. "I can't eat anything."

Lola took the tray from Annie, positioned it on the flat surface of the bedside table, and then said very firmly, "You have to eat. Starving yourself half to death won't get you out of this mess. Here, have some soup."

"I had something to eat yesterday."

Lola handed her a cup of chunky sweet potato soup and said in a coaxing voice, "Eat. And when you're done, I've got an idea for you. . . ."

Chapter Eleven

Evening in Jamaica came with quiet beauty. A blushing golden sky. A foaming dark blue ocean. An arc of parakeets frozen for an instant in the sky. But all of this went ignored by the group of people on the beach involved in a particularly boisterous game of softball.

"Run, Adam. No, the other way. The other way," Harry called out as the child pelted off in the wrong direction. "Don't worry; I've got your back, little man," Harry said as the child looked behind him as he ran. "Besides, your uncle Mik can't throw straight anyway."

Summer and Alana laughed heartily as Mik dived for the ball as it scudded across the sand, and missed it entirely.

Harry gave the plastic bat in his hand a couple of practice swings.

"OK. I was just warming up there. Now, check this. I'm going to hit this one right over Mother

Champagne's cottage. Adam, get ready to run again," he told the four-year-old.

Rob Champagne, a lanky twenty-one-year-old with tight curly hair and a face that held the promise of great masculine beauty, shouted, "Awright. Awright. I was just taking it easy on you. But see if you can handle this."

He went through an elaborate windup and then threw. Alana and Summer both ducked instinctively as the ball connected with Harry's bat and went whistling off in the opposite direction.

"Run, Adam," both Summer and Alana screamed as Mik and Rob scrambled after the ball.

Gavin, who was busy over the grill, stopped to watch his son tear around the two remaining bases. "Good boy," he called out as Harry high-fived the little boy.

Summer drew her legs up and leaned back on her arms. She shaded her eyes against the red-gold sun.

"Oh, there's Nicky now."

Alana turned to look. "He's got Amber, but no Amanda."

Summer rolled her eyes. "I've gotta talk to that woman. She just doesn't understand him, you know? A man like that you have to handle carefully. Ssh," and she put a finger across her lips as Alana drew breath to speak. "He's got ears like a dog."

"Dr. Alana Collins," Nicholas said as soon as he was close enough. "How are things in Guyana? I heard there was a truckload of rain and massive flooding in Georgetown." He bent to kiss Alana on the cheek and off-loaded his daughter from atop his shoulders at the same time.

"Come on, Amber sweetheart," Harry beckoned. "Your turn to bat. Let's show your uncle Rob what I taught you."

Nicholas flopped down on the sand next to Summer and Alana.

"Where are the cousins?" he asked after a bit.

Summer looked down at him. "Gone shopping in Ocho Rios." She reached across the blanket for her watch. "They should be back in an hour or two."

"Hmm," Nicholas said, and he lay back and closed his eyes.

Summer and Alana exchanged a glance, and then Summer asked, "What's this whole business about this Camille Roberts person and Harry?"

Nicholas opened an eye. "Oh. That."

Summer nodded. "Yes. That. Does he like the woman or something?"

Nicholas chuckled. "You've got to ask Harry that. You know what a bastard he is." He looked across at Alana and said, "Sorry, Lani. But you know Harry. When it comes to women, he's as steady as a drunken sailor."

Alana nodded. "I know my brother well." She couldn't be upset by comments like that. They were all true. Harry chopped and changed women as easily as most normal people changed their underwear. But maybe there was still hope. Nicholas had been quite similar. And now he was married. Settled with one woman. Maybe not happily . . . but . . .

"So, where's Mandy?" Summer surprised them both by asking.

Nicholas closed his eyes again. "Up at the house."

Summer poked him in the side. "What do you mean, 'Up at the house'? She's supposed to be down here, with us."

"Well, you tell her that, Summer, love. I'm just tired of the whole thing."

Summer uncoiled from her position on the blanket. This was getting serious. She knew her brother-in-law well, and she didn't like the sound of this at all. She walked across to where Harry and her husband were seated, reached into an ice chest for a pineapple soda, popped the top, and drank in one long swallow.

Gavin reached an arm for her and she settled onto his lap, her head resting against the curve of his chin. Harry looked at them both and said with mock remorse, "Now, if only I could find myself a good woman."

Summer laughed, and Gavin said, "What about this woman Nicky told me about? What's her name again . . . ?" And he looked at his wife.

"Camille." Summer nodded, eager to find out what the mystery was all about.

"That's right, Amber, hold the bat up high and just wait for it," Harry shouted, stalling for time.

Summer grinned at her husband. "Don't try to distract us, Harry Britton. What's the deal with this Camille woman? And why does she have to think you're a bum with not a nickel to your name?"

Harry smiled at her. "You know, you're just as nosy as my sister."

"Never mind that." Summer waved a hand at him. "Come on. Tell me. I can't get a single intelligent sentence out of Nicky. And Gavin knows what's up. I know it," she finished, turning to give her husband a loving glare.

Gavin shook his head. "Now see that? Harry, you'd better tell her before I end up sleeping on the porch tonight."

Harry chuckled, reached a hand into the ice chest for a beer, and then said, "OK. It's like this."

And he explained the particulars of what he intended to do, with Summer leaning forward with laughing eyes. When he was through, she asked, "But isn't that kinda mean, Harry? She might be a nice person, deep down. Why don't you just leave her alone if you have no serious intentions toward her?"

Gavin took a sip of his beer, grimaced as the bitter brew slid down his throat. "You've gotta admit, my beautiful wife has a point there, Harry. I mean, I'm all for a bit of fun. And God knows, the gold diggers of this world deserve all they get and then some . . . but you don't know this woman at all. She mightn't be nearly as bad as you think."

Harry's face tightened. "She might be even worse than I think."

"You know," Summer said, and she pushed a long swatch of black hair back from her face, "when Gavin and I first met, he thought that I was a gold digger. Didn't you, honey?" She gave her husband an innocent golden-eyed stare.

Gavin cleared his throat. "Well, I wouldn't go that—"

"He did," Summer cut him off. "In fact," and she leaned closer to Harry, "the only reason he went out with me in the first place was to teach me some sort of lesson. Didn't he tell you that?"

Harry exchanged a look with Gavin and said a tentative, "No. But I'm sure that's not true."

Summer folded her arms and said in a very smug voice, "Oh, it's true. Trust me. But I was ready for him, though. I bought myself the worst wig I could find, put on a really horrible outfit—"

"And don't forget the teeth," Gavin chimed in, his eyes gleaming with laughter.

Summer nodded. "Yep, I put some fake teeth in and wore some clumpy orthopedic shoes. By the time he showed up for the date, I looked so very pitiful that he felt sure I was about to keel over dead right then and there."

Harry guffawed. "Come on," he said.

"No. Really," Summer chortled. "He thought that I really looked that way, you know, without all of the makeup on. So, he had to back out of the whole

teaching-me-a-lesson thing, since I was such a pitiful creature."

"Yeah, she did some things to me all right,"
Gavin agreed. "She's just lucky that I'm such a nice
easygoing guy. I decided to make an honest woman
of her after a few years."

Summer gave Gavin a kiss on the cheek, said,
"Thank you, honey," then continued unbroken,
"Yeah, I bit him on the shoulder, too, and cracked his
head with my shoe. But that's a whole 'nother story."

Harry finished his final swallow of beer, wiped
his mouth with the back of his hand. "This Camille
Roberts woman is no Summer Champagne, though.
And you can trust me on that. She *is* an unrepentant
gold digger. A woman with no redeeming qualities
who—"

Summer rubbed her hands together and cut him
off neatly. "Sounds like love to me, Gavin honey.
What do you think?"

Gavin threaded a hand through his wife's hair and
spent a moment massaging her scalp. "Hmm," he
agreed. "We'll have to see. But since she'll be staying with us, there'll be plenty of time to find out
what kind of person she really is. We can't have
young Harry marrying just anyone at all."

Harry chuckled at that. Marry Camille Roberts?
That was a good one. If she was typical of most
women out there, and it was beginning to seem as
though she was, he wouldn't be marrying anyone at
all.

Chapter Twelve

"Excuse me, sir," Camille said for the umpteenth time. "Could you possibly move over just a little? You're sitting on my leg."

The large man seated beside her in the uncomfortable middle seat of the aircraft gave her a sour look. "And where would you like me to move to? The floor?"

Camille wiped a peppering of sweat from her brow and tried the kind of smile that usually bowled men over. "I'm sorry to be such a nuisance. But if you could just shift by just a little, I'd be fine."

It was just completely unbelievable that only three weeks before she'd been planning a life of luxury and relaxation. And in just an instant everything had changed. Now where was she? Trapped in economy class on a commercial airliner bound again for Jamaica. Lola's idea.

Camille looked out the window at the blue Caribbean Sea. She wasn't even clear on why she had agreed to the whole thing. A couple of months in Jamaica would clear her head, Lola had said. And Camille had agreed that a couple of months would. But, she had told her friend, she couldn't possibly afford to stay in a hotel for that length of time now. She just didn't have that kind of money. Lola had had a solution for that, too. Camille didn't need a hotel; she could stay with friends. The Champagnes.

Camille tightened the belt about her waist as the flight attendant announced their final descent into Norman Manley Airport in Kingston. The Champagnes. A thoughtful ripple creased Camille's brow for a minute. Who were these people who were suddenly such good friends of Lola's? Camille knew most of Lola's close friends, and the ones she didn't know personally Lola told her about. But Camille had never heard Lola mention these Champagnes. Except . . .

Camille forced her mind back over the days and weeks. Except that day when Lola was there helping her find a wedding dress.

Tears glistened in her eyes at the thought, and she wiped them away with a fierce hand. She wouldn't cry again. Wouldn't waste a single drop more of body fluid on Anthony Davis. He was a bum. A good-for-nothing bum. And he didn't deserve her tears.

As soon as the plane had landed and come to a complete stop, the interior erupted into movement. Men removing their bags from the overhead compartments, mothers comforting screaming infants, honeymooners kissing in the aisles.

Camille stood and trod heavily on the foot of the man next to her as she did.

"I'm sorry," she said at his dour look. Pins and needles still coursed through her half-numb left leg and she had to stamp it a couple of times to get the blood moving again.

"Sir? Sir? Can you help me get my bag down?" she asked a blond man who was somehow managing to weather the teeming and jostling crowd.

Camille wiped the sweat from her brow. Good God in heaven, she was in hell. Right smack dab in the middle of hell.

"Which one is yours, miss?" the man asked, peering around a screaming two-year-old.

Camille pointed to a compact brown roll-away made of good leather. "That one."

The man reached burly sunburned arms up, wrenched it down from where it sat, and handed it to her. Camille waved her thanks and joined the jostling line.

It took her fifteen minutes to get out of the plane and into the airport terminal. By then, her nicely cut green linen dress was damp with perspiration and loose strands of hair hung like overcooked spaghetti down the sides of her face. She inched her way through customs, told the officers that yes, she was an American citizen. Spent a few minutes more explaining the reason for her return to the island and then waited with veiled impatience while they scrutinized her passport and finally stamped it.

Camille rolled the suitcase out through the doors and stood on the lip of the concrete pavement, shielding her eyes against the bright sunshine. Lola had said that a woman would be coming to pick her up. Summer Champagne. The woman of the house. Camille had a general description of the woman. Tall. Maybe five foot nine or ten. Shoulder-length black hair. Caramel-colored complexion.

Camille looked around the parking area once and then again, slowly. A taxi driver bellowed across at her, "Need a ride, dawta?"

She waved the man away with, "No thanks. Someone's coming to pick me—"

And then she saw her. A tall, drop-dead gorgeous woman with long, beautifully waved raven hair and unusual brown-gold eyes. She was dressed in faded blue jeans and a white tube top. And was walking rapidly along the pavement, holding the hands of a little boy and girl.

Camille's eyes flickered over her. This had to be Summer Champagne. She walked with a certain confidence. A boldness. Hair swinging from side to side. Tiny waist moving with that unconscious sway that only certain women ever mastered perfectly. She looked like a pampered woman of wealth, of privilege.

Camille's mouth tightened. She knew for certain

that she wasn't going to like Summer. God, and she had agreed to spend two whole months in the woman's house. How was she going to stand it?

"Hello," Summer called out as she came closer. "You must be Camille. Say 'Hello,' Amber and Adam."

"Hello," both children chorused obediently.

Camille tried to smile. Great. Just great. The house would be full of screaming children, too. She was going to murder Lola when she got back. What could possibly have been going through her mind? It wasn't that Camille didn't like children. She loved them. But she had hoped to spend hours and hours of quiet time holed up in her room, thinking about her life. Figuring things out. How could she do all of that with two children running up and down wrecking the place? The house couldn't possibly be big enough to insulate her from that.

"How are you doing?" she asked, forcing a friendliness she didn't feel into her voice. She stretched her hand to shake, but Summer ignored it and instead swept her into a warm hug.

"I'm so glad you decided to come," Summer said in such a sincere manner that Camille was forced to give her another look.

"Oh . . ." Camille grappled for words. "I should thank you for . . . for having me."

"Pretty lady," Adam said, and then he hid his face in his hands and giggled.

Summer beamed at her son and agreed, "Yes. Very pretty lady."

Camille gave a shamefaced smile and pinched one of Adam's chubby fingers. "And you're a very handsome young man," she said, looking down into his unusual gold-colored eyes. He would be a lady-killer when he was grown; there was no question about that.

"And what about me?" Amber piped in, her huge black eyes framed by spiky lashes and a mass of curly black hair.

"Well, of course you're gorgeous, sweetheart," Camille said, turning her attention to the little girl. "Why, you must be a grown-up lady of what? Eleven?"

"I'm just eight," Amber said, but her face was wreathed in smiles.

"You've just made a friend for life." Summer grinned. "So, where are your bags?" she asked, looking around.

Camille tapped the roll-away with the tip of her designer shoe. "All I have is this one."

Summer raised nicely arched eyebrows. "Just one bag? For two whole months?"

The frown settled back into Camille's eyes. "Just one bag."

Summer's lips lifted in a little smile. Harry was going to have his hands full with this one. She seemed as prickly as a pear. But a certain amount of huffiness was to be expected. The poor woman had just recently called off her marriage. Summer was itching to know the reason why and would try to find out before the day was through.

"Well, if that's all the luggage you have, then let's get back to the car. It's sweltering out here."

They drove the distance back to Ocho Rios with Summer chatting lightly about this and that. Every so often, Summer would admonish the two children seated in the back.

"Stop quarreling, you two. And Adam, sit down right now. Don't make me stop this car."

Gradually, Camille relaxed and began looking around at the passing countryside. She had visited Jamaica only twice before, and on both occasions she had never left the resort. She sat back in the comfortable leather seat now and soaked it all in. The narrow twisting roads that wound their way through hills and valleys, giving her tantalizing glimpses of ocean through thick trees. The spindly coconut palms that grew in clusters at certain stretches along the way. The quaint colorful little houses that dotted the landscape, some tiny and crumbling in places. Others huge and magnificent with white wraparound verandas. She had never seen anything like it. And as they drove farther inland, she said to Summer, with slight amazement in her voice, "You know, I never thought Jamaica would look like this."

Summer gave her a smile and then honked loudly

as a chicken ran squawking into the road. "It takes you by surprise, doesn't it?" She nodded. "I've lived here for about . . ." And she wrinkled her brow in thought. "Wow, can you believe it? Almost six years now."

"Oh, really?" Camille was dying to ask more questions, but she didn't want to seem too curious.

"Oh yes," Summer agreed. "I met my husband, Gavin, in LA. I was working there as a designer. Then I was hired by his brother to do some work out here. And, as they say, the rest is history."

"A designer. In LA," Camille said in a flat little voice. So that was how Summer had managed to bag her husband. Maybe there was something to be said for becoming a career woman.

Summer flickered a glance in her direction and then returned her attention to the road. Camille wasn't overly talkative, but Summer would worm some details out of her yet.

"Adam, Amber, would you like some water coconuts?"

Both children answered with a resounding, "Yippee," and Summer asked Camille, "Do you mind if we stop for some? It's a little treat I always let them have when we go for a long drive. Keeps them calm, you know."

Camille looked at the two children in the back-seat. Adam was lying upside down with one foot poking at Amber's nose. And Amber was drawing a line of hearts on the leather of the side door.

A reluctant smile curved the corners of Camille's lips. "They seem calm enough," she said to Summer.

"These two?" And Summer raised her eyebrows. "Don't let them fool you." She glanced in the rearview mirror and hollered, "Adam. Stop that," as her son attempted to insert a big toe into one of his cousins' nostrils.

Camille turned away to hide the smile on her face. Children. You had to love them. She would've loved to have had a few, but . . . She sighed. That was a whole ball of wax that she just couldn't wrap her mind around at that very moment.

"I'll just stop here for a minute, OK?" And Summer pulled the SUV over to the side of the road, right next to a cluster of vendors. "Would you like anything?" she asked Camille. "The beef patties are especially good. And the coconut water is always ice-cold. Don't know how they manage to do it in this kind of heat. But it's one of the magical things about buying food from these roadside stands."

Camille gave the collection of wooden stands a dubious glance. God only knew what kind of bugs she might pick up if she bought anything there.

"No. That's OK. Really. I'm fine." Besides, she had never had coconut water before and wasn't too keen on giving it a try.

She sat in the car and watched Summer haggle back and forth with a plump woman who had a colorful head tie wrapped about her head. And marveled at the speed at which the woman chopped off the heads of the coconuts and then, with the tip of the long blade, bored a drinking hole in each chopped-off face.

The children returned to the car cradling the green-skinned coconuts and sipping on the water through a straw. They both climbed into the back-seat and sat there drinking contentedly until Summer returned to the vehicle with a bulging brown paper bag.

"Beef patties," she said, holding up the brown bag with a triumphant air. She slammed the car door behind her and then reached into the paper bag to re-move a crusty and very golden half moon–shaped pastry. "Sure you won't have one?"

Camille's stomach rumbled, and she hoped that Summer hadn't heard it. "No thanks. I'm really not that hungry."

Summer put the bag away and then sank perfect white teeth into the pastry. Warm, savory meat flowed into her mouth and she gave a contented, "Mmm." Then asked, "Adam, would you like a piece?"

"Yeth, Mom," The little boy nodded vigorously. Summer handed him a piece of hers.

Camille watched the child swallow the morsel, then waited for Summer to offer the little girl a piece, too. When Summer didn't, but continued to chomp on her patty, Camille asked with a trace of irritation in her voice, "What about Amber? Aren't you going to give her a piece, too?" She didn't believe in show-ing favoritism to one child over another.

Summer took another bite of the patty and said between chews, "Amber doesn't eat meat. Do you, Amber love?"

The child shook her head and said with a lilting Jamaican accent, "Eating meat is cruel, Auntie Sumsum."

"She loves animals," Summer said, and dusted her hands with a napkin. "Hasn't really ever been terribly fond of meat. We thought she'd grow out of it. But it doesn't seem as though she will."

Camille bit the side of her lip. How quick she had been to jump to the wrong conclusion. "So, Amber isn't yours, then?" she asked.

Summer started the SUV and moved back into traffic. "Amber is Nicky's daughter. Nicky is my husband's younger brother. The same one who hired me to come to Jamaica to work." She patted Camille on the hand in a very friendly manner. "Don't worry. You'll soon get your bearings. I married into the Champagne family, but let me tell you . . . these brothers are closer than most. It's one for all, if you know what I mean. My husband, Gavin, is the eldest of them all. And he raised the others almost single-handedly. He took them out of LA and brought them all here to Jamaica when Nicky began to get into trouble in South Central." A fond smile drifted across her face, and deep affection shone brightly in her eyes as she spoke. "You'll like Nicky. A more lovable rascal you'd be hard-pressed to find." She waved a speeding minibus around her. ". . . And of course, there's Mik, who's studying to become a doctor. And Rob, who's still finishing up college. Rob's a cousin. But he might as well be a brother." Summer gave Camille a glance. "And what about you? Are you leaving any family behind?"

Camille's hands tightened in her lap. "No family to speak of. I'm an only child, and my mother passed on a few . . . well, more than a few years ago. So," and she laughed in a sad little way, ". . . there's just me. And Lola. She's like a sister to me. She's . . ." Camille wiped at her nose with a quick hand as sudden tears rose in her eyes. God, what was the matter with her? Crying like this just because this . . . this Champagne family sounded so much like what a real family should be like. What was the matter with her?

Summer gave her time to gather herself and focused all of her attention on the road. Poor thing. She seemed so lost. Well, it was a good thing that she had decided to come to Jamaica. She would be able to find herself again. And whatever it was Harry was planning for her, Summer hoped it wouldn't be too harsh. She would talk to Harry about it, though. Her instincts told her that Camille Roberts, despite her prickliness, was a nice person. And Summer's instincts about people had not failed her yet.

Camille blew her nose on a white linen handkerchief she removed from her Gucci bag, and then said a slightly sodden, "I'm sorry." She rested an index finger against a temple and massaged. "I'm still in the crying phase right now. Any little thing can set me off." She stopped to clear her throat and then continued. "My wedding was supposed to be in about three weeks. But . . . it didn't work out."

Summer nodded. "I've been there."

Camille's eyebrows lifted. "You? But I thought you said that you were married to . . . to . . ."

Summer's golden eyes turned in Camille's direction. "Gavin."

"That's right," Camille agreed. "Gavin."

Summer slowed the SUV and eased in and out of a large pothole. "I was engaged to a guy called Kevin, before I met Gavin. Actually, I was still engaged to Kevin when I met Gavin."

"So, what happened?" Camille was really interested in hearing this.

Summer shrugged and said in a very casual manner, "I caught him with my so-called best friend. They were having a good old time in my bed."

Camille wiped the corner of an eye and said, "Oh." It was so similar to what had happened to her. But so very, very different at the same time. Her experience was much worse. Much worse.

Summer gave her a smile. "Girl, it was the best thing that ever happened to me. Every time I think about what my life might have been like without

Gavin . . . Without this family. Married to that piece of . . ." She glanced in the rearview mirror at the two children in the back. "I don't even want to think about it."

Camille chuckled, and the two women exchanged a look of understanding.

They drove on in companionable silence for a long stretch until the quiet was broken by a tortured, "Mom, I have to go potty."

Chapter Thirteen

It was midafternoon when they made the final turn onto the coast road in Ocho Rios. The day had turned so pleasantly windy that Summer lowered the two front windows and let the refreshing breeze blow right through the car. She swept a long swatch of hair back behind an ear now and said with a certain amount of relief, "We'll soon be home."

Camille looked about her with interest. There were tall trees with thick green leaves on either side of the road, and the trees sang beautifully as the wind raced through their leaves. She sucked in a deep, filling breath and then another. God, this was wonderful. Such quiet. Such peace.

"I can hear the ocean," she said, turning to Summer.

"Uhm." Summer nodded. "And you'll be able to see it pretty soon, too."

Camille gave her a genuine smile. Over the last couple of hours, Camille had been forced to revise her opinion of Summer Champagne. Although she was probably one of the most beautiful women Camille had ever seen, Summer wasn't hung up on that. In fact, she didn't even seem to be aware of it, somehow. She was warm, friendly, and . . . nice. And how could you not like someone like that?

"So, how far from the ocean is the house? I'm one of these ocean freaks. I love everything about it. The color, the smell, the taste."

"You sound just like Har—" And Summer stopped and bit hard on the side of her tongue. She'd been just about to say "Harry." Lordy. She had to be more careful.

Camille was looking at Summer with barely hidden curiosity, so she hustled into speech again, saying, "The house? It's right on the ocean. And most of the bedrooms have an ocean view."

Camille sighed. "Right on the ocean? That's wonderful. You know, that's what I've always—"

But what she'd been about to say was interrupted by, "Mom, I have to go potty."

Summer looked into the rearview mirror at her son. The last potty stop had had her hunting up and down a stretch of road for an appropriate bush, since Adam had refused to relieve himself anywhere else.

"Can you hold it for a few minutes, honey? We'll soon be home."

"I've got to go, too, Auntie," Amber piped in before Adam could reply.

Summer laughed in a rueful manner. "We're almost at the house now, darlings. So, would you prefer to use a bush or a nice clean toilet?"

That quieted them down for a bit, and Camille grinned at Summer. "I hope you don't have a flood in the backseat."

Summer gave both children a glance. "No. I think they're OK. They often imitate each other. If one wants something, then the other one does. Adam's older for his age because of Amber. And Amber's younger for her age because of Adam."

The trees began to thin out after another mile, and between them Camille could see snatches of clear blue ocean. For some ridiculous reason this simple thing made her feel happy. She rested her head against the leather headrest and allowed her mind to wander to Harry Britton. It had been a while since she had let herself think of him. But since she was no longer engaged to be married, who would it hurt? Besides, it wasn't as though she was ever going to see him again. Jamaica was a relatively small country, but even so, finding one solitary man, about whom she knew nothing, would be completely impossible. She would never see him again. But that was OK. He was a nice memory. And in her life so far, she had had so very few of those.

She sucked in another breath and caught a hint of sea salt on the air. Her heart picked up a notch. She would spend the next two months quietly regrouping. Getting things straight. Deciding which way to go. And who was to say? She might even feel like going back to Hedonism again. Maybe it was a place that Harry frequented. It was a long shot. But . . .

Summer turned the SUV into the nicely land-scaped entrance to the Champagne Cove estate and began crunching slowly up the pink gravel drive.

"We're here." Summer beamed. "Adam. Amber. Everyone OK back there? No puddles on the leather seats?"

"Oh, Auntie," Amber giggled.

Adam chortled happily, too, and the sound of their innocent mirth caused a warmth to settle right in the middle of Camille's chest. She rubbed the flat of her hand against the spot and muttered, "It must be gas." She should have had one of those beef patties.

Summer drove slowly by the front house. "This is where Nicky and Amanda live." And she pointed to the large multistoried house with its sweeping porti-coes and flower-strewn window boxes. "Mik and Rob also live there when they're down from school."

Amber tapped her aunt on the shoulder and said, "I live there, too, Auntie Sumsum."

Camille felt the urge to chuckle but quickly sup-pressed it.

"That's right, honey," Summer agreed. "You live there, too."

"I live there, too," Adam chimed in, not to be left out of things.

"You live with Daddy and Mommy in the manor house, sweetie," Summer corrected.

Camille looked around with some amount of amazement. "It's lovely." The place was simply huge. Much bigger than Lola's place in Maryland. And Lola had a big estate.

"There's a wonderful fruit orchard up through there." Summer pointed at an expansive outgrowth of trees that suddenly appeared as they rounded the bend. "In the evenings, I sometimes take a book out there, find a nice leafy tree, and just read for hours. There are a few cushioned benches scattered throughout, but I prefer to just sit on the ground with my back pressed up against a tree trunk."

Camille nodded and a certain melancholy drifted back into her eyes. This was the kind of life she could have had. Should have had. Maybe still could have? The Champagnes were obviously wealthy. And wealthy people always had wealthy friends. Summer was nice. Maybe she would introduce Camille around to a few eligible bachelors? Maybe this was the reason Lola had pushed so hard to get her here. That chick was a schemer through and through. And she would stop at nothing to get exactly what she wanted. But if this had been her grand plan, Camille would have to give her a big hug and kiss when she got back. If she got back.

Summer pulled into a parking bay where, Camille observed, there was a sleek little Mercedes-

Benz convertible and another SUV. She sucked in a breath and let it out. Now this was how she wanted to live.

"Come on, kids," Summer said as soon as they had come to a complete stop. "Let's get you taken care of. Camille, come on up. Mrs. Carydice will help you get settled. She's the housekeeper. I'll be right back." And she walked briskly across the drive and up the front stairs with the children following closely behind.

Just fifteen minutes away, in an apartment very close to the heart of Ocho Rios, Harry was in the middle of shoving a small collection of clothes into a duffel bag. He had been looking for various items of clothing for at least an hour and had finally decided to give up the search. The day before his sister had left for Guyana, she had decided to organize all of his things. Now he didn't know where a single thing was.

He opened a succession of drawers in his bedroom chest, rooted around a bit, and then slammed them shut again. Now, where in the name of heaven had Alana put his shaver set?

The ringing of the doorbell brought him out of his bent position, and for an instant he considered not answering it. He pulled the bedroom curtain back and peered out at the front stoop. His brows came together in a frown. Now what the hell was she doing here?

Francine Stevens adjusted her tight little skirt and waited as the lock on the front door was pulled back.

"Hi there," she said sweetly as soon as the door was open. "I brought you something."

Her eyes flickered over Harry as he stood big, tall, and unsmiling in the doorway. He had been avoiding her for weeks; she knew that. But he wouldn't avoid her today. It was silly anyway. She knew that he wanted her. She could see it in his eyes. The way he always tried not to look at her when everyone else was around. And wasn't she a grown woman now? Nineteen years old, no less. Her body was young and tight and all his to enjoy. So why was he fighting it? Sure, her cousin Summer thought she was a sweet little innocent. But truth be known, she hadn't been worthy of that description in years. Her first time had been with a boy from one of the local colleges. And she had been just sixteen years old then. A big sixteen. But sixteen nevertheless. She had sworn the twins to secrecy about the whole thing. And life had gone on just as before. But after a year or so of sweaty little clandestine meetings, she had grown tired of him and had gone on to someone else. There was always someone else. And now there was Harry. Her love. She wouldn't tire of him so easily. She knew that. And he could teach her so many things.

"Can I come in for a bit?" she asked when he still said nothing at all.

Harry cleared his throat. Now, how in the name

of God would he handle this? Summer had damn near threatened his life about staying away from her precious cousins. But how was he going to get this one to stay away from him?

"Look," he said, his face firm and unsmiling. "You shouldn't be here. Does your cousin know where you are?" He gave the covered basket in her hands a glance. "For that matter, do you know where you are? This is a nice little tourist town, but you can't just go wandering wherever you like whenever you get the urge. A little girl . . . ah, young woman like you in the wrong place could be snapped up in a second."

Francine smiled and placed the basket at her feet. "I don't mind being snapped up, as long as you're doing the snapping."

She advanced a step, and Harry was forced to take one backward.

"Now, Francine," he said, holding up a finger. "Whatever you're up to, I want you to stop it right now."

"Oh, come on," she said saucily. "You can't be afraid of . . . " she tilted her head and her voice took on an unmistakable Southern twang, ". . . li'l old me?"

Harry put a sofa between them. If this wasn't happening to him here and now, he might actually have found her little seductive routine funny. But it wasn't funny at all. What the devil was he going to do? Turn her across a knee and paddle her backside?

As freaky as she seemed to be, she most likely would enjoy that.

"Harry," Francine said with a tinkle in her voice. "Look at what I've got for you." And suddenly her dress was on the floor and she was standing there in nothing but her lacy white bra and panties.

Harry rubbed a hand across his face and said, "Jesus, this can't be happening."

She peeled back a bra cup, and cold perspiration sprang up across Harry's face. What could he do now? Run? Hide somewhere? Pray. He would close his eyes and pray.

He was so wrapped up in the problem before him that he very nearly jumped at the sound of a voice saying, "Well, well, Harry Britton. You'll never change, will you? But isn't she a little young for your tastes?"

"Janet. Janet Carr. I didn't know you were back in Jamaica." Harry came forward with outstretched arms and Francine was forced to drag her dress back up, annoyance written plainly on her face.

Janet gave him a skeptical look. "I got back from the U.S. yesterday. And I've been making the rounds. I brought you a little something, but I can see that you've got your hands full. So, I'll just come back—"

Harry reached a hand to detain her. "No. Really. Please stay. In fact," he said, looking at the girl who was still wiggling into her clothes, "you can do me a favor. Can you drop Francine off at Champagne Cove? She's a cousin."

Janet's brows lifted. "A cousin? Whose cousin? Gavin's?"

"Actually, she's Summer's cousin . . . so I guess that makes her your cousin, too. Francine Stevens."

Janet turned no-nonsense eyes in the girl's direction. "This is Francine? Sweet little Francine?"

Francine gave her cousin a speculative stare. She had heard all about Janet's story. Francine knew all the details, just like most people in the family. She knew how Janet had been abducted and brought to Jamaica by an old housekeeper. How Janet had been chasing after Gavin Champagne for years. How she and Summer barely got along. So Francine wasn't afraid of Janet. If she said anything to Summer about this, Summer wouldn't believe her. So there was absolutely nothing to worry about.

"Actually," Francine said now, securing the final tie on her dress, "I'll find my own way back to Champagne Cove."

Janet's eyes became like hot pinpoints of light. "No," she said, "you will drive back with me now. And when we get there, we're going to have a little talk with your cousin Summer."

Francine drew breath to speak, but Janet cut her off with, "Not another word about it. Or I can guarantee that you will be on the plane back to the U.S. by tomorrow."

Harry grinned at Janet. Women were so much better at this than men. Never, ever in his life had he been more pleased to see anyone.

"Hey," he said as Janet turned to go back through the front door. "Where's my gift?"

"In the car," Janet flung over her shoulder. "I'll give you it later. Maybe bring it by tomorrow."

Harry watched them through the window as they drove off. Francine Stevens was a complication he hadn't bargained for. He would have to be very careful now or the silly girl would blow the lid off of everything.

Chapter Fourteen

Camille was in the middle of hanging her clothes in the deep walk-in closet when there was a knock on the bedroom door.

"Come in," she said. "It's open."

Summer poked her head around the door. "Finding everything OK?"

"This is a beautiful room." Camille gave her a grateful smile. She hadn't expected anything like this. It was practically a suite unto itself. It even had a small sitting room with comfy aqua sofas and a flat-screen TV. And, of course, there was the balcony. A wonderful whitewashed masterpiece that wrapped itself around the room from window to window, providing spectacular views of the sea. She had opened up the French doors and gone right outside as soon as she had settled herself in the room. She had stood there pressed up against the balcony rails, just staring out at the ocean. Watching the endless ripple of waves as the wind blew across the water like an anxious father, hustling each rise of water

to shore and occasionally tossing a playful curl of
foam into the air in a handful of spray. She had
watched the beauty of it all with hard thoughts
churning through her mind. She would have to get
used to a life without massages and personal visits
from the beautician. Without most of the little luxuries she had become accustomed to. It would be this
way unless and until she found herself another man.
A wealthy one.

"I want to thank you again for having me here,"
she said to Summer now, her tone a little more for-
mal because she was vaguely embarrassed by the
fact that she wasn't paying for all of this comfort.

Summer waved the comment away and then
asked with genuine admiration as Camille placed a
slinky little dress on a hanger, "That's a Versace,
isn't it?" And she came into the room to ooh and aah
over the tight little number. She perched herself on
the edge of the bed as Camille continued to unpack.

"Oh, I forgot to tell you," and she picked up another fabulous dress, sighed over it, and then passed
it along to Camille to be hung in the closet. "I have
three cousins staying in the house at the moment.
Gavin took the twins, Diana and Deana, up to the
UWI today. That's how come I came to pick you up.
And there's Francine, too, the eldest of the girls. A
very sweet child. Prayerful. You know? She's hardly
ever at home. So, with the twins off at college, and
Francy out most of the time, I don't think any of
them will get in your way."

"That's OK." Camille smoothed a pair of jeans with her hand, placed them on a hanger. "I just hope I won't be any trouble to you and . . . Gavin."

Summer chuckled. "Don't be silly. We love having you here." She wracked her brains for the woman's name and then lied her head off. "Lola's a good friend of Gavin's, so when she said you needed to get away for a while. . . ." She shrugged and then galloped on to another topic entirely. "You'll meet Nicky tonight at dinner. He and Amanda come over every once in a while for meals. And every Sunday we all get together at somebody's house for Sunday dinner."

Camille was through with her unpacking and was sorely tempted to ask Summer whether or not she knew any nice, wealthy men whom she could vouch for. She didn't want to end up with another man on the *down low*. But God, in this day and age, it was so hard to find a straight man who was also a good man, who was also a single man.

She sat beside Summer on the bed, kicked off her strappy high-heeled Italian sandals, and massaged the ball of a foot. "You know, Summer," Camille began, and then she stopped as a tall figure loomed in the doorway. Her eyes met his across the distance and her body went completely cold. She knew this man. Had seen him somewhere before.

Summer looked up. "Nicky. Come in and meet our guest from America. Camille Roberts. Camille, this is the rascal I've been telling you about. Nicholas Champagne."

Camille's heart was beating in thick, uneven thumps. She knew this man. She knew this man. She knew this man. She wasn't very good with faces, but she remembered his. Most women would remember him. In the daylight, he was even more handsome than he had originally appeared. Tall. Lean. Classically handsome face. Curly black hair, a little longer than would be typically corporate. Deep black eyes. Her tongue flickered out to touch dry lips. Nicholas Champagne. Hedonism. Harry Britton. *That was it.*

Her eyes felt frozen and wide as she stared numbly at him. What was going on here? How did it come to be that this man was Nicholas Champagne? At the masquerade ball, she had taken him to be a gigolo. A party boy. Not one of the wealthy. Wait a minute. Wait one solitary minute. So, did that mean that Harry Britton was also wealthy? Her heart pounded at the thought.

She tried to breathe evenly. She had to be cool. She had to be.

"Hello there." He smiled and came forward to shake her hand. "Nice to meet you."

Camille swallowed. Her throat had gone bone-dry.

"Hello," she said, and little dimples appeared in her cheeks. "So nice to see you again."

Summer's eyes flashed to Nicholas, but his face gave nothing away.

"Have we met before?" he asked in a nicely modulated baritone.

"Well, we weren't formally introduced, but you were with your friend Harry at Hedonism a few—"

Summer's gasp interrupted her and Camille bit down hard on her tongue. Good lord. She had forgotten that he was supposed to be married. Now what had she done?

Camille stumbled into speech. "His car. . . ." She swallowed. "You were dropping him off there, remember? And I sort of ran into you both?" She lied with enthusiasm and hoped that he would back her up.

Nicholas gave Camille the kind of slitted-eye look that made Summer know that there was some lying going on.

Anger fired in her eyes. She had really thought all along that Amanda was being too sensitive about things. Had thought that Nicky was being faithful to her. Now, because of a perfectly innocent exchange, all had been revealed.

Summer's eyes were now a brassy gold in the setting sun. She was going to skin Nicky alive. Skin him alive. How could he do this to Amanda? How could he?

"Nicholas Champagne," she said in a tight little voice, "I'd like to speak to you outside."

A cool breeze was blowing in from the ocean, but Camille was sweating. What had she done? What had she done? What had she done? She waited for them to leave the room, and then she walked across to the bathroom to toss a handful of cold water into

her face. Lord, but she was slipping. It was just that
she had been so thrown by seeing him. So excited at
the prospect of maybe seeing Harry again that her
tongue had run way ahead of her brain. And now,
because of the clumsy lie she had told, Summer
might ask her to leave. She was obviously pissed.
God, why did things like this always happen to her?

She dabbed at her face with a towel and stared
into the mirror. She had to think. If Summer did ask
her to leave, she could stay in a hotel room, a cheap
one, for a few nights. She could use the time to track
Harry down. And if it turned out that he was wealthy
like his friend Nick Champagne, then . . .

An hour later Harry pulled up to the shack on the
beach, cut the motor, and rolled his motorbike out
along the creaky wooden walkway. The place was
just as bad as he remembered. He had bought this
little bit of beachfront from the Champagnes a year
or so before, intending to knock the shack down and
start over. Now he was glad he had waited.

He leaned the bike up against a stone pillar and
stood looking at the one-story place. It was a wreck.
But it was a perfect wreck. The paint was peeling. A
few boards were hanging off here and there. The
windows were filthy. But it was habitable. And that
was the important thing.

He walked around the entire structure, rattling
things, kicking at others. It took a few minutes to in-
spect the entire building, but in the end he was con-

vinced that it was indeed solid. He had had a contractor come out to have a look at it a week or so ago, and the man had checked out the structural aspects of the building. The place had passed inspection. But since Harry was planning on living in the shack for the next couple of months, he wanted to be absolutely sure that the thing wouldn't just collapse on him during the night.

He rattled the front doorknob now and a shower of dust and sand powdered the air. He brushed at his hair and then entered. It took a moment for his eyes to adjust to the light. And he moved the flat of his palm along the wall until it ran into a light switch.

He put his duffel back down. He hadn't paid that much attention to the amenities in the place when he had bought the land, since he hadn't intended living there. But from what he remembered, there was an outdoor toilet. No running water. A potbellied coal stove. And a solitary bedroom, which was separated from the living area by a dingy curtain of some sort. There was a tiny stand-up cubicle intended for bathing. But any such activity would have to be done with the use of a bucket.

He went to a window and looked out at the tangle of bush just beneath. It would take a lot of work to make the place look even halfway decent, but he would have the hellcat for help, so he wasn't worried.

Chapter Fifteen

Camille awoke to the sound of the ocean and she lay in bed for a long while just listening. There was something comforting about the waves. The constant ebb and flow. It helped her think. And for a stretch, as daylight came slowly, she let her mind just drift without worry. Last night had been interesting, to say the least. Instead of asking her to leave, Summer had returned to the room only minutes later to apologize. She hadn't explained what had passed between herself and Nicholas but instead had invited Camille down to dinner in the same warm and friendly fashion as before. And, after a moment's hesitation, Camille had followed her down. Dinner had been a cozy affair. She met Gavin Champagne and had marveled at how much he and Nicholas resembled each other. Gavin, though, was shorter than Nicholas, broader across the chest, and possessed a hard, square chin. There was a quiet strength about Gavin, and Camille knew instinctively that this was not the kind of man to play games with. She watched the interplay between him and his wife and knew a moment of pure envy. There was no question about it; Camille knew that this man loved his wife. And not only that, he loved her in a way that told Camille that he would never cheat. Never hurt Summer in any way.

And, with that realization, Camille had bent her head, tucked into the delicious meal of roast chicken, pearl onions, brown gravy, and candied potatoes, and tried to hide these feelings with pleasant chatter. But every so often, she would have to force a sigh down. She wanted the kind of love that so clearly existed between Gavin and Summer Champagne. So, why couldn't she have it? Why couldn't she find it?

Nicholas had not stayed for very long. And although Summer had coaxed him to bring Amanda and Amber back over for dessert, he had not returned.

Camille stayed on the deck talking until the wind developed an edge. She said her good nights then, went back upstairs to her bedroom, and for reasons she didn't care to investigate too deeply, cried herself to sleep.

Camille rubbed an eye now, yawned delicately, and sat up. Enough of this. She would have to stop all of this crying and carrying on. As far as she could see, she had two options. She could let this thing beat her, or she could fight it and win. And the night of sleep had given her back her perspective. She was going to fight. First things first, though. She would find out all she could about Harry Britton. And if he was unmarried . . . A shudder rippled through her. Funny. She had never once even considered the fact that he might not be available. What if he *was* married?

She walked out to the balcony in her shorty gown and stood there with the wind whipping through her hair. There was nothing to see but acres of sand and rocks and gorgeous blue ocean . . . and . . . She squinted at the approaching figure. An early-morning fisherman walking the beach with his net thrown across a strong brown shoulder. Her eyes followed the man. He was stripped to the waist, with a horrible floppy hat on his head, and was wearing a pair of ragged blue jeans. She shielded her eyes with a hand. He probably didn't know that this was a private beach. Oh well, let the poor man catch his breakfast, if that was what he was up to. She made to go back in again but turned when a voice hollered up at her, "Yo, lady. Want some fish for breakfast? I've got some nice mackerel and pink snapper here."

Camille looked down at the man and her brow wrinkled. Why in the name of heaven was he coming closer? Did she look as though she wanted any fish for breakfast? Who ate fish for breakfast anyway?

"No," she bellowed at him. "No fish. No fish."

"No fish?" the man shouted. He came closer still and Camille noticed for the first time that he was dragging something behind him in the sand. The fish, she supposed.

"That's what I said. No fish." Maybe he didn't understand English very well or something.

"How about some jewelry? I've got some nice coral." And he held up something that Camille couldn't quite make out. She pressed her lips together. This was ridiculous. She was going back in. And she would have to let the Champagnes know that there was a strange man on the beach selling things.

"Wait a minute," the man said as she turned to go. "How about some sex then?"

Camille's mouth plopped open. *"How about some sex then?" My God.* She had heard about the men on some of these beaches, but really. How dared he think that she would even consider having anything to do with him?

"Listen, you," and she bent lower across the rails so that he could hear her clearly. "This is private property. So if I were you, I'd get to stepping."

The man laughed, and it was something about the husky timbre of his voice that caused Camille to look at his face once and then again, hard. Her hand went to her throat and she said, "Oh my God. It's you."

Harry rolled the brim of the hat back so that more of his face was visible. So that was what Camille Roberts looked like without her mask. Not bad. Not bad at all.

"Well, hello there," he said, smiling up at her. "It's . . . the mystery lady from the ball, isn't it?"

Camille's chin tilted by just a little. Was he going to pretend that he barely remembered her? After all they had shared? "You know very well who I am." She had left him an extremely generous gift, too, so there was no way on earth that he could have forgotten her so very soon.

Harry shaded his eyes against the morning sun. "Of course I remember you, sweetheart. I remember all of my women. You look a bit different in the daylight, though. But, still, how could I forget *you*?"

Camille sucked in a tight breath. So, she had been right about him all along. He was a bum. Her eyes skimmed over his tattered jeans, floppy hat, and string of sand-encrusted fish. And to think she had actually hoped that he might be a man of means. What a joke. He probably scammed money off of the Champagnes and their guests whenever he could. And spent his nights doing the same thing to poor lonely women.

"That's a pretty interesting line of business that you're in. Selling fish, necklaces, and *sex*." She uttered the last word with a hard note in her voice.

He laughed again. "Oh, that. Well, a man's got to hustle. You know what I'm saying? Listen," he continued before she could even think of how to respond to that. "I've got a little place up the beach a stretch. Why don't you come over for a bite to eat? We can catch up . . . get reacquainted."

Camille straightened. "You have a place around here?"

Harry nodded. "Up that way. It's not as big as all this, but I call it home."

Camille's heart gave an unsteady thud. If he had a house around here, then that must mean that he had a bit of money. Her eyes grew thoughtful. But if that was so, then why was he wandering around the beach dressed like a homeless man, selling fish, necklaces, and only God knew what else? She was no fool. Something wasn't exactly right here.

"Is it your house?"

He shrugged in a careless roll of his shoulders. "Now it is. It used to belong to my parents, though. Long time ago."

Camille pursed her lips. Right. That made sense. God, what a wastrel. His parents had left him a beach house, but instead of using it to better himself in some way, he preferred to wander about the beach selling things he found in the sand. And to think she had wasted so much time dreaming about him. What a total and complete waste. But it was true to form, though. The way her life was going of late. She could almost scream. She had really hoped that by some miracle Harry Britton might have been the one to rescue her from the mess her life had become. But he couldn't help her. He could barely even help himself by the looks of things. It was just too bad.

"Thanks for the offer of breakfast. But I think I'll pass."

Harry tried not to laugh at the expression on her

face. She was eyeing him as though he were some particularly nasty form of bug life. But he would have her eating out of his hand, and soon. "Sure I can't tempt you? The fish is good."

Camille stepped back from the rails. "I'm sure."

"OK then. See you later."

She watched him walk up the beach with the sandy fish now slung across his shoulder. He was a damn sexy bastard, even in his bare feet and tattered pants. But she couldn't waste her time on him.

She turned and went back inside and then almost shrieked as something under the bed grabbed at her ankle. She whipped back the bed skirt and said, "Adam. What are you doing underneath there? You almost scared me half to death."

The little boy wiggled out chuckling. "Mom's looking for me," he said with wicked delight. "She wants me to take a shower, but I don't want to."

Camille sat on the bed and patted the space beside her. Once he had clambered up to sit, she asked, "You don't like taking a shower?"

Adam shook his head. "I told Mom that she didn't have to shower me ever' day, but she didn't believe me."

Camille laughed. What a boy. "You know," she said, running a hand across his curly top, "your mommy must be really worried about you. Wondering where you are. Don't you think we should go find her? She might be crying right now because she can't find you."

The little eyes grew wide and he asked, "Mom? Crying?"

"Well, she might be since she can't find you."

Adam gave Camille a steady gaze that made him look uncannily like his father. "But moms don't cry. Only babies cry. And sometimes Amber."

Camille stroked his cheek and was just about to dispute that when a knock sounded on the bedroom door.

Adam bounded from the bed and went scurrying for cover.

Camille uncurled from her comfortable position on the edge of the bed, wrapped herself in a soft robe, and then said, "Come in."

Summer poked her head around the door. "Sorry to disturb you this early. But you haven't seen Adam, have you? The little rascal's been hiding from me for the past hour."

Camille put a finger to her lips and then pointed at the bed. "No. I haven't seen him. I think he decided to run away to a place where little boys don't have to take showers anymore."

Summer nodded and said, "Oh well, I guess I'll just have to get myself another little boy then. Do you know of any nice little kids who like chocolate cake and ice cream?"

The bed skirt trembled, and then a head popped out. "I didn't run away, Mom. Here I y'am."

Summer chuckled and held out her arms. "Come here, you."

He darted straight into his mother's outstretched arms, and Summer swept him up, kissing him soundly on each cheek. "Now, boyo. Time for your shower."

Summer waved a few fingers at Camille and with Adam snuggled against her neck said, "Mrs. Carydice has breakfast ready. I wasn't sure what you'd like, so I asked her to make a little of everything. Toast. Juice. Eggs. Bacon. Go down whenever you'd like."

Camille took a long refreshing shower, toweled herself dry, and then sat on the lip of the tub to do her toenails. She dried her hair next and spent long minutes seated on the pretty pink and white bench that sat before the dressing table. She braided her hair in one long plait, creamed her face, and then sat for a moment, thinking. She had been rude to poor Harry Britton. It wasn't his fault that he was a wastrel. Some people were just born that way, without any ambition. But still that was no reason to treat him the way she had. She would have to take a walk over to his house to apologize.

She finished dressing quickly and let herself out of her room.

"Oh, good morning." She smiled at Gavin Champagne as he passed.

He was carrying a rolled-up newspaper underneath an arm, and he stopped for a moment to talk pleasantly about a few of the sites that she might like to visit in Ocho Rios.

"I was actually thinking of heading up the beach," she told him. "I . . . ah, received an invitation from your neighbor this morning, so I thought I'd drop by his place for a bit."

Gavin nodded. "So you've met Harry then?"

"He was walking on the beach earlier this morning," Camille said. "He's very friendly."

"Oh yes," Gavin agreed. "Harry is that. Well," and he slapped his thigh with the newspaper, "have a nice time. If you need anything, just let Summer know. She'll take care of you."

Camille thanked him and then trotted down the long staircase to the first floor. Breakfast was laid out buffet style on a long side table, and she took a peek under each silver dome before deciding on a simple meal of jam and toast with steaming hot coffee.

She was helping herself with a white breakfast plate in hand when the housekeeper appeared to ask, "Would you like some pineapple juice, miss? Or maybe some coconut water?"

Camille turned and said very pleasantly, "Oh, thank you. But I'll just have some coffee, please. Two milks and a little sugar."

She took her plate out to the deck and sat at a poolside table. It was a windy day, and the sleekly shaped black-bottomed pool appeared almost navy in the sunlight. She crunched on her toast and let herself just enjoy the morning.

"Auntie. Auntie."

Camille turned in her chair to see Amber come sprinting out to the deck area.

"Look at what Daddy and Amanda got me." She came to a scudding halt as soon as she realized that Camille was not her aunt.

"Your auntie's still upstairs, sweetie," Camille told her. "But what've you got there?" She looked down at the child's cradled arms and saw the chocolate brown fur of a spaniel pup.

"It's a puppy." Amber beamed. "Isn't he sweet?"

"Uhm," Camille agreed. And then she feigned confusion. "But where are you going to keep him? Is there enough room for him, too? I've heard that you've got a lot of animals."

Amber giggled. "I only have two doggies so far. And a cat called Ruggles. So there's enough room for him."

Camille stroked the silky little head, and the puppy opened a sleepy eye, licked her on the hand, and then went promptly back to sleep.

"See," Amber said with a joyful note in her voice. "He likes you. My daddy says that dogs only like good people."

Camille laughed. "Well, I'm sure he's right. So, what are you going to call your puppy?"

She tilted her head and considered the question with great seriousness. "Do you think I can call him Amber Junior?"

The housekeeper came out with a steaming mug

of coffee, and Camille thanked the woman before saying with the same degree of seriousness in her voice, "Hmm, Amber Junior. Well, that's a nice name. Definitely a nice name. But isn't he a boy? A boy should have a nice, strong boy's name. Shouldn't he?"

Amber thought on it again with eyes squinted almost closed. "Butch," she finally said. "I'll call him Butch."

"You'll call who Butch?"

The voice behind them caused Amber to turn with a squeal. "Auntie Sumsum. Look."

Camille smiled to herself as Summer fussed over the puppy and the little girl. What nice people. Nice children. They really deserved all of this opulence. She blinked rapidly. She was going to cry again; she just knew it.

She heard Summer send Amber inside and picked up her coffee mug and drank deeply. Summer came across to sit, and Camille wiped a bead of moisture from the corner of her eye and asked, "No breakfast for you this morning?"

Summer wrinkled her nose. "I've been feeling queasy of late in the mornings. I just hope I'm not pregnant again."

Camille gave her a startled look. "You don't want any more kids?" The idea of someone not wanting an entire houseful of children, especially when she could afford it, absolutely threw her.

Summer looked down at her nails. "I really don't

know. I had a hard delivery with Adam. But that's not really the crux of it. Amanda, Nicky's wife, has been trying for the longest while to have one. And . . ." She spread her fingers.

Camille nodded. "Oh. I understand. Hmm. You know," and she leaned forward, "there's a surefire way for Amanda to get pregnant. It works all the time."

Summer's eyebrows lifted. "Really?"

Camille nodded. "Really. But I'll have to tell you all about it later." She glanced at her watch. Where had the morning gone to? It was almost ten.

"Going exploring?" Summer asked as Camille stood.

"Just up the beach. Thought I'd take a look around."

Summer watched her go with a smile. She was going to Harry. Good. Very good.

Chapter Sixteen

Camille cut through the living room and headed straight for the front door. She sat on the stairs for a bit to adjust the lace of a sneaker, then stood, dusted the back of her shorts, and trotted down the stairs. She was severely tempted to take a quick walk through the orchard, but after a moment's thought she decided against it. She had plenty of time to look around. Maybe one afternoon she would take a book out there and just sit and read.

She walked in the direction of the ocean, enjoying the rustling pull of the wind. If it were completely up to her, she would live by the sea for the rest of her life. She had had her fill of the city, the parties, the socials, the bars. She just really wanted a nice quiet life. A life with children and family and good friends. She wanted to be able to wake up every day and know that, yes, this was where she lived. This was where she belonged.

Camille skipped down the stone stairs to the

beach, stopped to pick up a small orange-pink shell, inspected its soft white underbelly, and then tossed it away again.

She walked on with head slightly bent, hands jammed into her pockets. Of course being able to afford a massage and a half a dozen other such luxuries every now and again wouldn't hurt, either. But being able to walk on the beach every morning and go to sleep with the crash of waves every night was really, if she looked beyond everything else, what she wanted. No, needed.

A playful wave rushed out toward her, and she felt the urge to chase it. Once when she was about eight, maybe ten years old, her mother had taken her out to Rehoboth Beach in Delaware. It was one of her best-remembered memories of childhood. And one of the few days off her poor old mother had had.

Camille frowned at the sand. Working that way, day in, day out, until your body finally said "enough." *That* wasn't what life was all about. Surely human beings weren't put on this earth in order to work themselves into early graves?

Tears filled her eyes, and she wiped a hand across her face and sniffled. Her mother had done her best, though. She had worked that way so that her only daughter could have a better life. A much better life.

Camille looked out at the horizon at a passing cruise ship. It seemed huge and majestic, even at this distance. She sighed. If only her mother could have lived longer, she could have gone on cruises, too. But that was all history now. And what had already passed couldn't be changed.

Camille wiped the round of her nose, sniffled again, and continued up the sand. When she was eighteen years old, her mother had said to her, "Cam, I want you to do much better than I've done. Promise me that. Promise me you will." And she had looked at her daughter with eyes that were already beginning to dim, and Camille had promised her that she would do better. But she had also promised herself that she would do it without working herself to death.

She sniffled. Money. Sometimes she really, really hated it. It was the root of all evil in the world. It turned people like her into something they were not. Something ugly and cheap and superficial.

She glanced back over her shoulder. The manor house was quite a distance behind her now. She shaded her eyes. The sun was getting hot now. She could feel the burn on her shoulders. Maybe she should have brought a hat with her. But she hadn't thought that Harry's house would be this far up. And she knew that she was heading in the right direction, too, because this was exactly the path he had taken earlier in the morning.

She stooped to catch the break of a wave in her hands and patted the water against her face. It was good. Not cold but some beautiful temperature that she couldn't quite articulate. She breathed in a deep and luxuriant way. Ahhh. If only life could be like this all the time.

She continued up the beach, following the curving trail of sand and rocks and sudden blue-green pools. The coastline meandered in the most peaceful way, bending this way and that. And suddenly, around a cluster of boulders, there was a house. It was perched on a promontory of thick rock, and Camille was caught off guard by its quaint beauty. The face of it was covered by a profusion of climbing yellow-gold roses, and a huge wraparound veranda provided a perfect view of the sea. It was a wonderful little place and not at all what she had been expecting.

She looked down at her bare legs and sneakers. She looked decent enough. Besides, he had invited her over. So it wasn't as though she were just bursting in on him.

Camille dusted a bit of sand from the side of a leg, straightened the run of her shorts, and then began the climb up the wooden stairs to the latticework veranda. She gave the front doorbell a firm ring and stood back. He'd be surprised to see her, given her rude treatment of him earlier. But she would think of a way of explaining all of that to him. She could say that it had been early, that she wasn't a morning person, that she hadn't slept well.

Or she could just go for the truth. Apologize and go for the truth.

Footsteps behind the door made her heart begin an unsteady thumping rhythm. Here it was. Here he was. OK. She was ready.

The door opened and Camille couldn't avoid a startled, "Oh." She stared at the slightly plump older woman. So, he lived with his mother then?

"Oh, what? I'm trying to sleep and you're ringing and ringing my doorbell like that. Don't you have any home training at all?" the older woman asked, and she gave Camille a beady-eyed look.

Camille tried a wide smile. "I'm so sorry. But is Harry at home?"

The woman was unimpressed. "What?"

"Harry Britton," Camille tried again. "Does he live here?"

"Uhm-hmm," the woman said, as though it all made sense to her now. "You're one of Nicholas's girls, right? Look at you, the way you're dressed. Skin. Skin. Nothing but skin. Probably came over to get a little something. Right? A little roll in the sack? A toss in the hay? Well, I've got something fo' you. That's right. Don't look so surprised. I got something fo' you."

And she reached beneath a table next to the door to remove a hibiscus stick still carrying a few un-plucked leaves. Camille took a hasty step back. "Listen, ma'am, I think there's been some sort of a mistake here. I'm looking for Harry. Harry Britton."

"Don't you sass me, miss."

From somewhere in the bowels of the house there was the sound of running feet, and then a woman dressed in a nurse's uniform appeared.

"Oh, I'm sorry. So sorry, my dear," and she hustled the older woman from the doorway. The nurse stopped to catch her breath and then returned to say, "I was downstairs doing some laundry. I left her sleeping, but I guess the doorbell must have woken her." She extended a hand. "I'm the nurse. Nurse Robbins. I look after Esther Champagne. She's the mother of them all, you know?"

Camille didn't know and at that moment didn't much care. The whole thing had unraveled with such unpredictable speed that she found herself groping for words. What in the world had just happened? Was the woman completely out of her mind?

"She wouldn't have hurt you at all, you know, dear. She's not violent."

Camille took a shuddering breath. Well, that was debatable as far as she was concerned. *My God.*

"I was looking for Harry Britton's house. I guess this isn't it?" *Please, God, let this not be it.*

Nurse Robbins wiped her hands on a towel hanging from about her waist. "Oh, Harry. Isn't he up at the house?"

"No. He passed by this morning. But he's not there now."

"Ah," the nurse said. "Well, maybe he's in Ochi then. Would you like to come in for some lemonade? No? Well, I'll just get back to my washing then."

And she was gone from the door before Camille could say very much else. She turned away and went back down the stairs to the beach.

So, the Champagne mother was mentally disturbed. Poor thing. And she'd just been feeling so very sorry for herself and thinking how lucky all the Champagnes were to have such an idyllic home with every little material thing that they could ever want. Jeez. In life, you just never knew sometimes what was going to happen. There was always something wrong somewhere. Either you had all the money in the world, but the man was on the down low. Or you had hardly any money at all, but the man was as sexy as all get-out. It was never perfect. Never perfect.

She squinted ahead at the glistening sand. Whew. It was going to be a hot one today. Well, she would walk for a bit longer, and if she didn't see the house, she would just turn back around. Go back to the manor house and take a nice long dip in the pool. Maybe play with Amber and Adam for a bit and then see if she could help out with Amanda Champagne's problem. Because getting pregnant, if you knew the right techniques and if you used the right herbs, was not a problem at all.

The sound of a dog barking in the distance made Camille turn and smile fondly. Little Amber and her dogs. What a sweet child. Camille rounded another swell of jutting rocks, looked up at the cliff side, and said, "Oh my God."

There was a house there. Well, barely a house at all. It was more of a ramshackle lean-to, covered with thick vines and what might be centuries of blackened grime. It was a horrible little shack, and the sight of it made fresh tears spring to her eyes. Harry just couldn't live there. Surely this wasn't his beach house?

She considered turning around, going back the way she had just come. But the sun was scorching hot now, and even the breeze blowing in from the ocean didn't quite seem to cut through the heat. Besides, she needed to use the ladies' room, and there was no way on earth that she was going to go back to Esther Champagne's house and use the facilities there.

Camille looked up at the rock face. Of course there would be no stairs leading up to the place. Why had she even thought that there might be some?

She propped her hands on her hips. Well, she needed to go to the bathroom and there was no way that she was going to stoop behind a rock to do her business, so she was just going to have to climb the thing. It didn't look that difficult. There were nice smooth places where she could put her hands and feet. And not such a bad drop to the sandy beach, just in case she lost her footing.

She looked down at her sneakers. Good thing she had had the presence of mind to wear them.

She walked to the base of the cliff side and shouted, "Harry. Harry Britton." But her voice was carried away on the wind.

She placed one leg on a rock, tried the sturdiness of it, and then bent to climb. Slowly, hand over hand, she clambered up the slope. Every so often a shower of sand rained down into her hair, but she kept going nevertheless. Somewhere near the top of the climb, she heard the *thunk thunk* sound of chopping. She froze where she was on the slope, with her ear turned to listen. What if this wasn't Harry's house, either? What if this was the Champagne father's house? Whoever was chopping up there obviously had an ax. And if the father was also a little unsteady in the mental department, she would be in a whole heap of trouble.

She turned to look over her shoulder at the sand below. God, her bladder was full to almost bursting. But maybe she should go back down. Because the way things had been going for her of late, the man up there who was doing the chopping was quite probably a lunatic of some sort who had taken refuge in the ramshackle house. She looked below again and then decided. Yes. Right. She would go back down.

She shifted her grip, shuffled a foot sideways.

Now, how in the world was she going to manage this without falling flat on her rear end? It was so much easier to climb up the face of the cliff than it was to go back down it. She stopped to listen again, and her heart lurched. Oh God, the chopping had stopped. What if she was right? What if—oh no. He was coming this way. Maybe if she squeezed herself flat against the side of the cliff . . .

Heavy footfalls clumped above, and more sand and debris rained down. Camille tried to smother the desire to cough. But the dust. The dust was going to make her . . . She sneezed. Loudly.

The footsteps stopped. Clumped back to directly above her. Then an amused voice said, "Well, well. So you decided to come over after all?"

Camille wiped the side of her sandy face against a shoulder and peered up at him through one eye. He was leaning over the side grinning all over his face.

"Would you help me up?" she croaked after clearing her throat a few times.

He reached a hand down and hauled her up the rest of the way.

"You know," he said after she had brushed herself free of a good quantity of sand and twigs, "it's much easier to use the stairs. Unless of course you were just out getting your daily dose of exercise?"

Camille pressed her lips together. So, he had a sense of humor, did he? No ambition but a sense of humor nevertheless. Well, if she were in his position in life, she wouldn't find all that much to laugh about. Living in a ramshackle house that by the looks of it was about to fall into the sea.

"You know very well that there are no stairs leading up to the top of this cliff from the beach," she said. "Otherwise, I would certainly have used them. I'm not some sort of a maniac."

Harry pointed toward the right side of the house. "Didn't you see that?"

Camille followed the line of his hand. "You don't mean that . . . that rope thing?" He certainly wasn't calling that piece of rope running up the cliff side stairs, was he?

Harry picked up the ax and slung it across a shoulder. "It's a darn sight better than scrabbling your way up the hillside. There are grooves carved out of the rock face all the way to the top, so all you have to do is just hold on to the rope and pull yourself up and—"

Camille lifted a hand to stop him. *Whatever.* She had no interest at all in the whole thing. What she needed to do, and fast, was find a functional bathroom. "Listen," she said. "Do you have a bathroom I can use? It was a long walk over here from the manor house."

Harry shifted the ax. "Bathroom?"

And the degree of puzzlement in his voice made Camille ask, "You do have one, right?"

He scratched the side of his head. "Yeah, I've got one, but I'm in the process of fixing it up. It needs a bit of work. But if you don't mind."

"I don't mind," Camille said, and tried to avoid shifting from foot to foot. Whatever it looked like was perfectly fine with her. After all, how bad could it be? As long as she could sit down somewhere and then flush, she really didn't care at all about how attractive the place was.

Harry gave her a flickering look. "Come with me then."

Camille hurried after him and tried not to notice the black grime on the outside of the house. The place was in really, really horrible shape. What was left of the external paint was warped and peeling. There were boards hanging off here and there. Most of the windows were without glass. And if that weren't bad enough, the house itself was canted at a drunken angle. It was a wreck of a house. In fact, it was a kindness to call the thing a house. It looked more like a badly constructed shed than anything else.

Camille wrinkled her nose and stepped around a pile of foul-smelling dirt. Where in the name of heaven were they going? They had already passed what appeared to be the front door of the shack. And given the pathetic size of the place, it would make no form of sense to have a back door. Her brow beaded with perspiration. Maybe he had misunderstood her?

"We're almost there." And he turned his head to smile at her.

"Harry," she began, but before she could finish what she was about to say, they had rounded the back of the house and he was saying, "Here we are. Now remember, don't squat too low over the hole. A colony of red ants seems to have moved in there over the last several days. And they bite."

Camille looked at the shed, at Harry, and then back at the shed. An outdoor toilet? An outdoor toilet where she would have to squat down over a hole filled with vicious biting ants? Was he completely stark staring out of his freaking mind?

"I'm not using . . . that . . . that thing," she told him. "A hole in the ground with insects and other things in it? I can't use that. I've never used anything like that before and I just can't use it. I can't."

Harry rested the ax against the side of the house. "Well, that's all I have. So if you really need to go . . ." And he gave a little shrug.

Camille sucked in a breath. Maybe she could hold it. Maybe if she ran really fast, she could make it back to the Champagnes' house.

He reached up into an overhanging piece of roof, felt around for a moment, and then took down a white roll of kitchen paper towels. "You might need some of this." He tore off some paper. "Think you'll need more than a few squares? I can't afford to waste any of it, you know?"

Camille shifted from right leg to left and back to right. She couldn't make it back to the Champagnes'. She just couldn't make it. "Just give me that." And she snatched the paper he had just torn off the roll, darted into the corrugated zinc shed, and slammed the door closed.

From outside, she heard him yell, "Careful you don't fall into the hole. And don't forget to throw some dirt in when you're done."

Don't fall into the hole. Don't fall into the hole, Camille fumed. It was as black as hell in the place, and she could barely see half an inch in front of her own face. And what did he mean about throwing dirt in when she was done? He was crazy if he thought that she would be picking up anything and throwing it into a filthy hole in the ground.

She danced on the spot as her eyes adjusted to the lack of light. And gritted her teeth as he began to whistle. She couldn't understand it at all, but the lunatic was happy. He was actually happy living in these appalling surroundings.

She moved gingerly over to the hole in the ground, looked around for any potentially vicious insects, and then with quick fingers pulled her shorts down.

Outside, Harry bent his head against an arm and laughed quietly. The look on her face when he had shown her where the bathroom was, was almost worth all of the trouble he had gone through to get her here. Jesus, but he was going to enjoy himself.

A clang and a muffled swearing from within the shed caused him to call out, "Are you OK in there?"

Camille considered not answering him but told herself that she was being childish. It wasn't his fault that he was as poor as dirt. "I'm OK. I just hit my foot against this . . . this pail in here. But I'm fine."

She shuffled to the door, opened it, and was grateful for the immediate shot of sweet ocean breeze. Jesus in heaven, she hoped that she never had to do that again.

"Did you throw the dirt in?"

Camille gave him a hard look. She was sure he was laughing at her but couldn't for the life of her figure out why that was. "No, I did not throw any dirt in. Never in my life have I ever had to flush a toilet by throwing some dirt in it. And I'm too old now to start. So, if you want any dirt in that . . . that hole, you're just going to have to do it yourself." She looked around for a pipe or any sign of running water and sighed. It had been too much to hope for that there might be some water somewhere. "Is there anywhere to wash my hands?"

He gave her a considered, "Hmm," and then pointed to a covered drum that had been shoved against the side of the house. "You can use some of that. There's a ladle, and some soap." He pulled off some more paper and thrust it at her.

Camille washed her hands quickly and tried not to be too aware of the fact that he was just standing there watching her. Out of the corners of her eyes she could see the pure artistry of his body. The hard, sleek lines. The beautiful ripple and pull of perfectly conditioned muscles whenever he moved. Lord, but he was a good-looking man. What a waste. What an absolute waste. And the thing about it was that he seemed really intelligent. If he put his mind to it, really put his mind to it, he could probably do well in some type of business. Maybe something in sales. Then he could afford to fix his place up or just sell the land off to a developer or someone like that. Oceanfront property was at a premium everywhere in the world.

She dried her hands on the paper and turned to find that he was still watching her, and now with a slightly puzzled expression on his face. "What's the matter?"

He rubbed a hand down the flat of his stomach. "You surprise me. That's all."

Camille followed him around to the other side of the house and waited for him to pick up a few pieces of wood before asking, "Surprise you? How?"

He stacked some more wood beneath an arm. "You're a society lady, aren't you?"

"Society lady?" Now what did he mean by that? Did he know something about her?

"I mean, you're one of these rich American career women I read about all the time. Aren't you? And yet you didn't kick up too much of a fuss about having to use an outhouse."

He stacked the wood in his hands against the side of the house and then went back for some more. "You know what I mean?"

Camille had no idea what he was talking about. If she had to go, then she had to go. And raising a fuss about the bathroom facilities would have been totally pointless as far as she was concerned. It wasn't as though he had presented her with another option. "Well, I always manage regardless."

"Hmm," Harry agreed. She was obviously made of sterner stuff than he had originally thought. But she hadn't seen the inside of the house yet.

"I didn't give you my name last time we met," Camille said, changing the subject because it made her a bit uncomfortable.

Harry smiled. "That's right. You never did. So, what is your name, mystery lady?"

His smile was so wickedly infectious that Camille couldn't help smiling, too. "Camille," she said. "Camille Roberts." And she waited for the barrage of questions: What had all of the mystery been about then? And what about the night they had spent together? Did she just go around picking up strange men in hotels? And, by the way, how did she come to be staying with the Champagnes? How did she even know people like that?

But he just busied himself with stacking more wood against the house and didn't ask a single thing.

"Well, aren't you going to ask it?" she said after it became clear that he wasn't going to question her at all.

Harry picked up the final armful of wood. "Ask what?"

Camille pursed her lips. Now he was just being obtuse. He knew very well what. "Aren't you surprised to see me here? Staying with your friends the Champagnes?"

Harry clomped up the three stairs leading to the front door, pushed it open, and beckoned her with, "Why don't you come in? The sun's beginning to get hot. Don't want you keeling over with sunstroke." He left her query about the Champagnes alone.

Camille followed. She wasn't altogether keen about going into the house. Was it even safe? "You don't have any of those biting red ants inside there, do you?"

Harry laughed and the deep, hearty sound he made caused a ripple of sensation to course the length of her spine.

"No ants," he said. "But you'll have to sit on cushions. I don't have any chairs." He gave her a quick look. "I don't do very much entertaining here."

Camille closed her eyes and told herself that she shouldn't expect too much. He wasn't a rich guy. He couldn't afford very much, what with his current occupation of selling sandy fish and trinkets on the beach.

She opened her eyes and gasped. *Oh my God.* It was even worse than she had thought it might be. It was like the inside of a barn, with cushions of all sizes and descriptions just tossed around at random. And in the midst of the chaos, shoved beneath a plastic-covered window, was what appeared to be a soot-covered witch's cauldron.

Camille looked across at Harry and struggled for something nice to say. She had heard her grandmother talk of pots like the one beneath the window, and since it was arguably the best item in the entire place, she seized on this. "That's an . . . antique cauldron, isn't it? Looks about what? Nineteenth-century? Somewhere there? Must be very valuable." She nodded her head to show him that she wasn't judging him.

Harry coughed loudly, because the urge to break into laughter again was strong.

Camille bit the inner curve of her lip. It was no wonder at all that he had a cough like that, living in a place like this one. No running water. A witch's cauldron for a stove. And biting ants for company.

Harry cleared his throat. "It's a coal pot actually. They work very well, you know. Might take a bit longer than the electric models, but the food tastes pretty much the same once you're all done."

"Hmm," Camille allowed. There was no way on earth that she would ever marry a man who expected her to cook on one of those. Her poor mother would turn in her grave.

Camille looked about for a place to sit and chose a large square cushion of indeterminate color. She checked the floor around her for ants before perching on the edge of it.

Harry lit a kerosene lamp and then walked about the small space, opening windows.

Camille watched him for as long as she could manage to control the words and then blurted, "Can't you get a job?"

Harry turned, genuine surprise on his face. "What's that?"

"A job. A job. Can't you get one?"

He walked across to the coal pot, peered in, then stirred the contents.

"Well?" Camille prodded when he didn't answer her immediately.

"Why should I want a job? I have all I need right here. The sea gives me food. The trees give me wood. I collect rainwater. I have everything I need."

Camille's mouth worked soundlessly as she thought of how to respond to that. How could he be so damned complacent? Didn't he want more? Didn't he have any goals for himself? Didn't he at the very least want a decent place to lay his head every night? How could he say that he had it all? He had nothing. Nothing at all. And what was tragic was that he didn't even appear to realize it.

"But what do you mean?" she pressed. "You . . . you visit your friends the Champagnes all the time, right? They have running water in their houses. They have electric lights. Cars. Other things. Don't you want any of that?"

Harry stirred the pot again and then beckoned her over to taste.

Camille clambered off the cushion and went across to give the concoction in the pot a dubious look. "What is it?"

Harry rubbed a hand across the base of his chin. "I'm not so sure about that yet. I can tell you what's in it. There's fish. Vegetables. Some seaweed. That's good for you, by the way. And this time I tried adding a few mangoes."

Camille's stomach churned. "And you want me to taste it?"

"Please." He dipped a generous portion and held out the spoon.

Camille looked at the spoon. She should just tell him that she wasn't going to have any of it. But somehow, she didn't have the heart to do it. He had probably spent all morning brewing the mess. The least she could do was take a little taste. "Put a little in my hand," she instructed. "A little. I said a little."

Harry poured the entire spoonful into her hand

and waited with the expectant air of a master chef.
Camille hesitated before bending to take a little of
the concoction in her mouth. She swallowed in an
awkward, clenching motion. It was terrible. Just terrible. And what was she going to do with the rest of
the stuff in her hand? She was just going to have to
tell him. That was all. She was just going to have to
tell him.

"Well?" Harry raised both eyebrows. "Pretty
good, huh?"

"No." Camille shook her head. "It's no good. I
don't want to hurt your feelings, because I know you
worked hard on this. But it's truly the worst, the absolute worst, thing I have ever tasted."

Harry cleared his throat and asked with innocent
eyes, "The worst thing you've ever tasted? Come on.
Maybe if I stir it up for you. Most of the good stuff's
in the bottom anyway. Here, let me try. . . ."

"No. Really," Camille stopped him. "It's no good.
And even if you stir it all day, it'll still be no good."
In fact, the stirring might actually make it worse, if
that was even possible.

An idea occurred to her, and before she could talk
herself out of it, she said, "Look, why don't you let
me whip something up for you?" She didn't want to
be immodest about her culinary abilities, but she
could burn. And by the sounds of that cough of his,
it would be a very good thing indeed for him to get
some decent food into his stomach. If this was what

he usually ate, it was a miracle that he hadn't keeled over dead already.

"You'll cook? For me? On this?"

She seemed to have surprised him again, and Camille said, "I mean, don't get me wrong. None of these . . . ah, cooking things are ideal, but I'll manage, somehow. Now," and she was suddenly businesslike, "throw out what's in the pot. And find me a table or a board or something for me to cut on. Get me a pan of fresh water. A knife, and make sure you wash out that cooking spoon." She didn't want the taste of what he had cooked spoiling her pot. "And if you've got it, bring me some flour, and any seasonings you have."

For the next hour, she rattled off instructions. And very soon the house was filled with the smell of good cooking. She sliced the remaining fish down the center, removed the bones, and then cut it into slabs. He did have half a bag of flour and a few eggs, so she made a tasty batter, dipped the fish, and then placed everything to simmer in the big pot with a few dabs of butter he removed from what appeared to be an ice cooler.

Harry sat on the floor and watched her as she busied herself about the place, throwing open more windows, opening up the door, peeling and then chopping ground vegetables. She was like a whirlwind, and he was deeply surprised. Shocked even. He had taken her for a completely useless piece of society flotsam. A social butterfly who probably didn't know one end of a kitchen from the next. But strangely, inexplicably, there was more to her. This required further investigation.

"Is this what you do for a living?" he asked her now.

Camille chopped a thick sweet potato root into neat squares, opened the pot, pushed the fish aside, and put the pieces in to fry.

She wiped her forehead with the inside of an arm. "Do what for a living? You mean, cook?"

"Uhm-hmm," Harry agreed. "You seem pretty good at it. Almost like a professional."

Camille turned a slice of fish before saying, "Can't every woman cook? It's a pretty basic skill. Mothers teach their daughters, and those daughters teach their own. And so on and so on."

"So, you're not a professional chef then?"

Camille laughed. What an idea. A professional chef? "No, I'm not a professional chef. Just a good cook." If she did say so herself.

Harry leaned back on the cushions and stretched his legs before him. "So, what do you do for a living then?"

Camille lifted out a crisply browned slab of fish and rested it on a swatch of paper towel to blot the excess oil. Now why did he have to ask her questions like that? What was she supposed to say? That she did nothing at all for a living? That she had made her way so far living off of the generosity of men?

She frowned. What did that make her? "I . . . I haven't really settled on a career yet."

"So, how do you make your money then? Are you independently wealthy?"

Camille lifted out more fish. She could see very well where this was going. He was probably going to suggest that she look after him. A quid pro quo arrangement of sorts. Wasn't he ashamed? A big, strong, intelligent man like himself?

"I can't afford to take care of you, if that's what you're angling for," she said with a snappy note in her voice.

Harry threw back his head and laughed. "Take care of me?"

Camille shot him an angry look. "I don't see what's so funny. That's what you do, isn't it? Scam wealthy women for whatever they'll give you? What you should really do, if you ask me, is get yourself a job. You're too damned intelligent to be wasting yourself this way. What do you think your poor dead parents would have to say about it if they could see you now?"

Interest shone brightly in Harry's eyes. His poor dead parents? And was she lecturing *him* about working? About what she thought he did for a living?

"But you don't work, do you?" he asked, all innocence again.

Camille pushed the sweet potato cubes around in the pot. What did that have to do with anything at all? Wasn't she trying to explain the benefits of honest toil to him? Why did he have to bring her into the matter? Did she live in squalor? In a building that probably should be condemned? "I don't have a job, at the moment. But that has nothing to do with what we're talking about."

Harry shrugged. "Well, if you don't work, then why should I? What's the difference anyway? As long as I can eat, and I have a place to sleep, why should I stress myself with a nine-to-five occupation? Working that way takes up too much time. See what I mean?"

Camille released a tight breath. No, she most certainly did not see what he meant. What she did see, though, was that he was a bum. A pure and simple bum.

She tried a different approach. "If you continue like this, what are you going to do when you get married? How will you support a wife and family?"

Harry crossed his arms behind his head and relaxed onto them. "Maybe I won't get married. I'm perfectly happy the way I am. Why should I mess up a good thing?"

"Of course," Camille agreed. "You think that makes sense now. But it's a selfish attitude, and believe me, selfishness reaps its own reward in the end."

Harry chuckled at that, and Camille gave him a

hard look. "Where are your plates? Or don't you have any?"

"There're a couple of calabashes in the corner. You can use those."

"A couple of what?"

Harry leaned up on his elbows. "Calabashes. You know what they are, don't you?"

Camille propped her hands on her hips. "No. What are they?"

He uncurled from his position on the floor and went across to the corner to lift two round containers. "A calabash," he said, holding one up. "It's a gourd, basically. They grow on trees around here."

Camille sighed and took them from him. She wasn't going to say anything else. Not a word more. If he wanted to live in this horrible manner, eating out of gourds and cauldron pots, then that was completely up to him.

She put two pieces of golden-brown fish, a generous helping of fried sweet potatoes, and an assortment of other vegetables into the deep belly of the calabash and handed it to him. "There's nothing to drink of course." And quite probably nothing to use as a drinking utensil.

Harry rested his calabash on the floor. "Wait a minute. I do have something here." And he went across to the ice cooler to remove a large coconut and then another. "They should be ice-cold by now."

And before Camille could tell him that she didn't

want any coconut water, he disappeared outside. She settled herself on a cushion, propped the calabash between her legs, and waited for him to finish chopping the heads off the coconuts. If she had any of that coconut water, her stomach was going to run; she just knew it. Her system was delicate. She wasn't accustomed to living a ramshackle life.

He returned a few minutes later, with coconuts in hand, and Camille said in a slightly apologetic manner, "I should have told you before you went to all that trouble. I can't drink that."

He set a nut down before her. "Why can't you drink it? The water is cold and sweet." He tilted his head back, swallowed a good quantity of coconut water, wiped his mouth on the back of a hand, and said, "Ahh. Good. Come on. Try it."

"I really can't." She pressed a hand against her stomach. "My body doesn't take well to foreign things."

"Have you ever had coconut water before?"

Camille took a bite of fish. "Nope. Never had."

"So, you've made up your mind with absolutely no information? That's closed minded."

"Closed minded? Me?" That was a joke. She was the least closed-minded person around, and that was the truth. She put the calabash down and grabbed the nut. "OK. I'll have some of the water in this thing. But I'm telling you, if I come down with stomach flu or something, you're going to have to carry me back to the Champagnes' on your back, because I am not using that . . . that shed out back again."

She took a small taste of the water and ran her tongue along the soft inner nut. Well, it did taste quite good. Not oily or strange tasting at all. Cold and very refreshing.

"Well?"

Camille rested the coconut at her feet. "It's good."

"What was that?"

Camille smiled. "OK. OK. It tastes very good. Satisfied?"

"For the moment."

Chapter Seventeen

It was early evening when Camille finally decided to go. It was strange how quickly the day had disappeared. After they had finished lunch, she had helped him clean up the place a bit. She had given the body of the house a good sweeping out, had taken all of the cushions out to be aired, and then had started on what remained of the glass windows, wiping and washing and then wiping again. The bedroom, a mere cubbyhole as far as she was concerned, was swept out as well and the dingy curtain hanging by the doorway taken down, washed, and hung out to dry.

She had had no intention at all of doing any of this when she arrived earlier in the day, but after she saw the conditions in which he lived, her heart went out to him and she had to do it.

"I think I'll bring the cushions in," she said now. The sky, which had been a bright blue all day long, had turned suddenly gray. And a strong wind laced with a wet edge rolled in from the ocean, gushing through the windows and dousing the flickering kerosene lamp.

Harry went about the house shutting windows and battening down the thick sheets of plastic that hung in place of broken-out glass. "It's going to rain," he said. "Let me help you with those."

Together, they carted everything back inside. And Camille spent a moment tastefully arranging the cushions, hanging the freshly washed curtain. She stood back to look at her handiwork when she was through. The room looked worlds better. A few more curtains, some chairs, a center table, and it would almost look like somewhere to live. Almost.

"Not bad." Harry nodded. "Not bad at all. I have to give you something for all of this."

"Trust me," Camille said with a little laugh. "You couldn't afford to pay me."

Harry advanced. "Is that right?"

She nodded and stood her ground. He was going to kiss her, and she was ready for him. In fact, if she was being strictly truthful, she had been ready for him from the first moment she saw him walking on the beach.

"So, what are you going to do?" Her eyes were playful.

"What do you want me to do?"

They both laughed at that. Camille's eyes sparkled at him. What a man. It was such a pity that he was an unambitious bum. How could he possibly expect a woman to live in a place like this, even if she was willing to overlook the fact that he couldn't afford to buy her any of the finer things?

Harry rested his forehead against hers. "This is what you get for surprising me." And he kissed the left corner of her mouth. "This is what you get for cooking such a delicious meal for me." Warm lips found the right corner of her mouth.

"Don't forget the cleaning part," Camille said, tilting her lips up closer to his. "I've got to get something for that, too. I don't work for cheap."

Harry settled his lips against hers, and Camille sighed. This was what she had needed all these many weeks. Lying alone in her bed at night, she had needed this.

He kissed her softly, gently, and she opened to him like a flower, giving him more and more access until they were straining against each other, struggling to get closer. She moved a hand across the bulge in his pants. God. She was already aching for him. But she couldn't. Not here. Not in this place.

"I have to go," she gasped, tearing her mouth from his.

"Stay." And he rubbed his mouth against her ear, pulled the fat of her earlobe in to suckle. "Stay."

Camille shuddered. It was so tempting. So very tempting. But she couldn't. She couldn't. Harry Britton, no matter how sexy, no matter how entertaining, was not the right man for her. He wouldn't even work, for God's sake. No. She couldn't stay. Because if she did, if she only did, it would be hard, so very hard, to tear herself away, once she did find another man.

"No. Really. Stop. You have to stop."

He turned her face toward him again and devoured her lips, sucking first on the top one and then on the bottom. Camille groaned in reply. Why did this man have such a strong and powerful effect on her? Why him? He was a bum. A bum, for pity's sake.

The sky was rattled by a jagged flash of lightning, and he held her closer, wrapping both arms about her. "Stay with me. Just for a little while."

"The Champagnes . . . dinner. They'll be wondering where I am," she struggled for the right words that would keep him under control. Keep her under control.

"We'll call them afterward."

"Call them afterward?" She was so hot she could barely think straight. "You have a . . . a phone?"

Harry rubbed a hand between her legs. "Cell phone. Everyone in Jamaica has one."

"Ah . . ." she said, and shifted to give his hand better access. What could it hurt? Just one more time? She wasn't promising him anything. He wasn't promising her anything. No one could possibly get hurt.

He seemed to sense that her resistance was all gone, and Camille bent her legs willingly as he lifted her with ease and walked the short distance to the bedroom. She closed her eyes as he placed her on the flat mattress. She couldn't believe she was doing this here. Now. He didn't even have a sheet on the mattress. It was just a bare contraption of cloth and springs and foam, with none of the silky frills she always insisted on. Oh. She couldn't do this. It was ridiculous. Insane. But so good. So good. She couldn't stop him. It was impossible to stop him now. After they were done, she would get up and go back to the manor house, and she would not see him again. That was the only solution. But she couldn't stop him now.

Harry removed her shorts without Camille even realizing that he had done so. Outside, a roll of thunder brought her eyes back open. It had begun to rain, and the plastic sheet across the window flapped madly in the wind. But Camille found that she didn't even care about that anymore.

She opened her legs, guided his head down, and then lay back in golden contentment as he feasted. Nothing. Nothing in the world was better than this. Nothing. Not even money and cars and diamonds . . . well, maybe diamonds.

She grunted as he pulled her short nub of flesh into his mouth and rolled it around between teeth and tongue. No, this was better than diamonds, too. Jesus. How was she going to say no to this if he came after her again? How was she going to say no even if he didn't come after her?

He pulled her down and without further prepara-tion, entered her. She bit his shoulder, but he held her firmly in place and moved to the rhythm of the rain on the plastic sheet. Her fingernails curled into the flesh of his back, and she became like a tigress. Strong and fierce and greedy. Her legs wrapped about his waist, holding on. Rocking with him. Eyes closed. Tongue pressed into one corner of her mouth. She matched him move for move, thrust for thrust. He called out for her, and she answered him with wild strangled cries of her own. There was nothing else. Nothing else. Nothing else.

She felt the wet of rain on her cheeks, or maybe it was her own tears; she didn't know. And still he rocked, and still she matched him. The mattress shifted, reared up at the head, bunched itself against the wall. And he held her firmer still, pulling her legs up. Moving. Thrusting. Rocking. Groaning.

She opened her eyes to stare at his face. Laced her fingers with his. Muttered his name. Cried out as the beauty took her and then sighed in utter content-ment when it took him, too.

Later, with the steady patter of raindrops on the corrugated zinc roof, she slept. And Harry held her while she did, curving his body about hers to keep them both warm. His mind was a blank. An utter and total blank. And that had never happened before. It was as though she had wiped him clean. Completely clean. God, but she was good in bed. He'd had many women in his life. But never one who had managed to satisfy him as she did. He didn't have to chase the pleasure when he was with her. It was just there. Omnipresent.

He closed his eyes after a good long stretch of listening to the rain, and he slept. But this time he locked an arm and a leg about her. She wouldn't escape him again unless he wanted her to.

At about eight o'clock his cell phone rang and Harry answered it with a sleepy, "Britton."

Camille opened satiated eyes and listened to him as he talked. His laughter rumbled in her ear, and she felt a sudden and totally unexpected shard of jealousy. Who was calling him at such an hour? It had to be a woman. Camille could always tell when a man was speaking to a woman on the phone. His tone changed. It grew softer, more accommodating.

She shifted to get away from his leg, but he hauled her back to him so that she was forced to lie there and wait until he was finished with his call. Her temper was beginning to rise by just a little when he said, "OK. I'll talk to you later then."

He snapped the phone closed and shifted Camille around to face him. "Summer," he said. "Wanted to know if you were still here."

The slight frown on Camille's face relaxed. Oh. Summer. She had thought it might be someone else. But why did she even care, though? What did it matter if he had other women? She was just being silly. "I didn't hear you tell her that I'd be there soon."

He shifted up onto an elbow. "Why would I tell her that? You're staying the night."

Camille sat up and Harry's eyes went straight to her well-shaped bosom. "I'm not staying the night." What if she wanted to go to the bathroom, which was more than likely? There was no way that she was going out to the shed in the back in the middle of a tearing rainstorm.

Harry bent his head and took a broad-tipped nipple into his mouth. Camille's toes curled in response. No. No more of this. She had to go. She just had to.

He suckled the nipple with just the right degree of pull and played with the stiff tip of the other. Camille closed her eyes. Well, OK, maybe just once more.

Chapter Eighteen

Harry took her back to the manor house the next day. After the third satisfying session of lovemaking, Camille had decided that there was no point in trying to make it back home in the rain. Her legs were like rubber and there was a lassitude in her muscles and bones that just did not allow her to take a single step away from the warm cocoon of his arms and legs.

She slept well. Breathing deeply. Dreaming sweet undisturbed dreams. And somewhere on the edge of morning she turned to sling a leg across his hips and snuggle deep into the curve of his neck.

Harry awoke to find her wrapped all around him, and he kissed her softly on the neck. If he hadn't already decided that she was definitely not the right woman for him, well . . . there was no point in thinking about things like that. He had no interest in getting married. And even if he did, he wouldn't marry a woman like Camille Roberts. She was entirely unsuitable. There were much better women around. Women who would know how to conduct themselves in civilized company. Women who weren't money-hungry superficial little gold diggers. No. He didn't want her. He would cure her of her problem, that was it, and then let her go.

Camille awoke to find him staring at the ceiling with a very stern look on his face. She touched him on the side of his jaw, and he turned to say, "You're awake."

Camille stretched in a long and lazy movement of arms and legs. "Well, you wake up in a great mood," she yawned. "The rain's stopped."

"Uhmm," he said. "When you're ready I'll take you back to the manor house. You can take a bath here or just wait until you get there if you prefer."

The smooth skin between Camille's eyebrows developed a kink. What was the matter with him now? Men could be so strange and unpredictably moody sometimes. At least when women were moody, there was a very good biological reason for it.

She rolled away from him. "I'll get dressed." She would wait to bathe at the Champagnes'. Because she certainly wasn't looking forward to a bath with a bucket of ice-cold water.

Harry dragged on his pants. For some unknown reason, he was in a totally uncharacteristically foul mood. He needed a bath. A good one with hot water and soap. He needed a sink and a mirror so that he could shave.

"Do you want breakfast?" he tossed over a shoulder as she slipped her top on and pulled up her shorts.

"Why don't we go out for something? I'll pay. And you can show me the town."

"I don't have the time today."

Camille pressed her lips together. So he was determined to wallow in his foul mood. Well, she wasn't having any of it.

She followed him out into the living room. "Look," she said. "If you're worried that I'll be hanging about the place here, messing up the time you spend with other women, you don't have to worry. In fact, if we hadn't slept together last night, I wouldn't even be here now."

He frowned at her. "What are you talking about?"

She propped her hands on her hips. "Well, what's this mood all about then? If something's bothering you, why don't you just come out and tell me? I'm not a freaking mind reader."

Harry rubbed a hand across his face. She was right. He was behaving like an ass. "I just need a hot bath. That's all."

Camille's eyebrows lifted. "A hot bath? That's why you're in a mood?"

"I'm not in a mood."

Camille made a disbelieving sound. "I told you yesterday that what you need to get is a job. If you had a steady source of income, you'd be able to afford to get running water, hot and cold, in this place. But you have your own ridiculous ideas about that."

"And what about you?" he shot back. "Why are you drifting about the world from one luxurious destination to the next? Isn't that a pretty pointless existence?"

Luxurious? Pointless? The poor lunatic had never had a taste of that kind of a life, so he had no idea at all what it was he was missing. "Luxury isn't pointless. For many people it's the entire point of their existence. The reason they work themselves half to death. The reason they get degrees, open businesses, struggle, and sacrifice. It's all for money and the luxuries it can buy."

"Well, why don't you work then, since you like this kind of life so very much?"

She crossed her arms before her. "My mother worked, and worked pretty damn hard. You know where all of that got her?"

Harry gave Camille a steady look. "Where did all that get her?"

"Nowhere. Nowhere at all. When she died she didn't have a single thing to show for it."

"She had you to show for it."

"I mean money. Money. She had no money to show for it. After all those years."

Harry turned away and went to the bucket of water to wash his face. "There's more to life than money, sweetheart. Much more."

She followed him. "Well, you try to survive without it and see how far you'll get."

He said nothing at all in response to that, and she

stood there watching him as he washed his face, brushed his teeth, and then shaved.

"Pour some of that water over the back of my neck," he said, pointing at a pail of water on the ground. He leaned forward over the makeshift sink and waited expectantly.

Camille picked up the bucket and poured. It was absolutely ridiculous. Ridiculous. What was she even doing here? This man couldn't help her, damn it. Had she completely lost her mind? Lola would be shocked, shocked, if she could only see her now.

"That good enough?" she asked when the bucket was almost empty.

Harry scraped a hand through his hair and reached for the remnants of what used to be a towel. "Yeah. That should do it."

She washed her face and scrubbed her teeth next and did what she could with her hair. When she was through, she went back to the living room area and found Harry seated on a cushion, putting on his shoes.

"I'll run you back over to Champagne Cove."

Her eyebrows lifted a bit. Run her back over there? How? "Oh, do you mean you'll take me back across there on your shoulders?"

Harry laughed. His good humor had been completely restored by the quick wash. "You're quite the comedian, hmm?" He grinned.

Her lips twitched. "Well, what else could you mean? Do you have a car?"

He stood. "A bike. If that's good enough for you?" He laughed again at the questioning expression on her face. "It was a gift. OK? A gift."

"Hmm," Camille said. And she sat to replace her sneakers. How could he be satisfied with this sort of life? Accepting handouts from women? Little gifts of this and that? Sure, women did it. She did it. But that was different. It was expected that men would give things to the women they liked. They'd been doing it for centuries. And there were good, solid historical reasons behind the custom. But it wasn't the same for men. Men, by tradition, were expected to be able to stand on their own two feet. Pay their own way through life. It gave them self-respect. Self-worth. It made them men.

"I'll wait for you outside, OK?"

Camille nodded. He was as happy as a lark again, she could see. But his head was as hard as a stone. Why couldn't he understand the importance of having material things? Why couldn't she get it through his thick head that he should work for a living? There was joy in that. There was accomplishment in that.

She finished tying her laces and stepped outside. A wonderful breeze picked at her hair right away, and the sudden glare of bright sunlight blinded her for a few seconds. She shaded her eyes and called, "Harry?"

"Over here."

She followed the sound of his voice and found

him standing beneath a large leafy green tree. "What are you doing?"

He reached up to pluck a red-gold fruit from a low-hanging branch of the tree.

"Breakfast," he said. "There's nothing like a good ripe mango in the morning." He massaged the fruit and then handed it to her with, "Try it. Come on," he said when she gave the mango a very doubtful look. "You're not a fruit snob, are you?"

"I'm not any kind of a snob."

She rubbed the skin of the mango on her shorts and then bit. It was warm and juicy and sweet and very, very good. She closed her eyes and sighed. God. This was living. The ocean. The wind whispering through the leaves. Hot sunshine almost all the time. She could stay in Jamaica forever. It was a beautiful place. But to do that, she needed money. Damn money again.

Harry watched her as she ate, his eyes flickering over her smooth forehead, pert little nose, soft lips. She was a beautiful woman; there was no question about that. And maybe it was part of the reason that she had been able to take the easy path through life. But a woman who was intent on marrying for money needed to be much more than merely attractive to the male eye. She had to be intelligent, too. Very intelligent. She had to be able to convince the poor love-struck man that she really loved him, too. And since Camille Roberts had managed to land some poor sucker, it meant that she had the requisite amount of gray matter. But that was perfectly OK. He was more than up to the challenge. In two weeks, she would be eating out of his hand. And in three, she would have sworn off wealthy men entirely.

Camille finished eating her mango and asked, "You're so quiet all of a sudden. Is another foul mood coming on?"

Harry chuckled. "Just thinking."

"About what I said?" She tossed the mango seed into a clump of brush. Ordinarily she was opposed to any form of littering, but in this kind of heat she knew that the seed would grow into another tree in next to no time at all.

He smiled at her. "What you said? Oh, you mean about the getting-a-job thing? No, no, I wasn't thinking about that."

She made a sound of irritation. "What did you do with that necklace I gave you, by the way?" She'd been itching to ask him the question since yesterday.

"Necklace?" And he looked at her as though he had no idea at all what she was talking about.

"You know what I mean. The chain I left you at Hedonism."

"Oh, that."

Camille's expression grew turbid. *Oh, that? Oh, that?* Did he have any idea how much the chain was worth? On the black market, it would probably fetch at least five thousand U.S. dollars. Was he a freaking half-wit or what? "Yes, that. What did you do with it?" If he had any sense at all, he would have pawned it, sold it, used it as collateral for a loan or something.

Harry tossed his mango seed into the bushes, wiped a streak of juice from the corner of his mouth with the back of his hand.

"I gave it away."

"You gave it away?" Camille gasped. She shook her head. "You gave it away." She was speechless. Flabbergasted. Just about ready to slap him senseless. He was as poor as the proverbial church mouse, but he had still seen fit to give away five thousand dollars.

"I gave it away. It was just a worthless trinket, wasn't it?"

"It was not . . ." And Camille was forced to take a breath. "It was not just a worthless trinket. I never ever give worthless trinkets away as gifts." She gritted her teeth and counted slowly to ten. There was no point in getting upset. No point at all. He had given the chain away, and that was all there was to it. "You know what you need?" she said, looking at him now in a very straight and steady manner.

"Tell me."

"You need someone to look after you."

And he looked at her with such dumb innocence shining in his eyes that Camille felt like grabbing his shoulders and shaking some sense into him. Where was he living anyway? In the Land of Oz? This was a cruel world they were living in. A hard and cruel world. And it had no time at all for fools or innocents. Which one of the two he was she wasn't exactly sure.

"And don't smile at me like that, either. You . . . you . . ." Great big idiot. Anyway. Anyway. She couldn't deal with it. She just couldn't deal with it. Besides, it wasn't her affair. If he wanted to give away everything he possessed, then let him. The damned fool.

"Let's just go." She'd had enough. More than enough.

Harry chewed on his lower lip. She was hopping mad. And all because of her little diamond-encrusted chain. When he was through with her in a month or two, he would give it back. She'd probably need the money then.

They walked around to the front of the house to where a motorbike stood. Harry handed her a helmet, strapped his on, and then kicked the bike started. Camille climbed on behind him and wrapped her arms about his middle. She didn't like these kinds of bikes at all. They were narrow and dangerous and always ended up killing somebody or other. "Are you sure we'll be safe on this thing?"

"Don't worry," Harry yelled above the noise of the motor. "I haven't lost a passenger yet."

"Well, that's nice to know." And she clung to him tightly as they started off along the bumpy track that led to the road.

In a few minutes, they were tearing down the main road, with Harry bent low across the handles and Camille bent along with him. It was amazing how very well he handled the bike. He dodged holes, went into dips, came out of them, and rode the undulations in the road with complete mastery. After a short few minutes, Camille lost her fear of falling off and was able to enjoy the ride. The wind was fierce but sweet, rushing into her hair, pulling at her clothes, making her feel wild, free. It was fantastic. Liberating. And over far too soon.

They were at the entrance to Champagne Cove in about five minutes, and Harry turned in.

"I'll wait for you while you take a shower and get a change of clothes."

"What was that?" Camille screamed to make herself heard.

"I'm taking you to Ocho Rios."

The bike was making too much noise for any more conversation, so Camille absorbed the change in plans in silence.

He came to a stop outside the manor house and waited with both feet planted for Camille to climb off. She removed the helmet, handed it to him.

"I thought you had something else to do today, it being Saturday and all?"

He shrugged. "I can take care of that tomorrow. So, run upstairs and take your shower. And bring a swimsuit with you."

Swimsuit? He really was taking a lot of things for granted. First he blew her suggestion of a meal off, and then just as arbitrarily he now wanted her to go along with him to this Ocho Rios place. She should just tell him that she wouldn't go. That *she* had important things to do.

"So, why are you standing around?" He glanced at his watch. "I want to get into Ochi before it gets really crowded, and you know how long you women usually take to fix yourselves up."

Camille turned on her heel and headed for the steps. "I'll be at least half an hour," she tossed over her shoulder. Maybe she'd be an hour or even longer. It was never a good thing to just fall in line with a man's plans. Especially when he came up with them at just a moment's notice.

She pushed the front door and tried not to give in to the urge to look at him again. She knew that he was still sitting there on his bike watching her. And she didn't want him to think that he had her in any way. He didn't have her. And a man like him would never have her in that sense. Sure, she could play with men like him, but never anything else. *Never anything else.*

Camille trotted up the stairs to the second level, grateful that there was no one else around. She wanted to slip in, get a steaming hot shower and a change of clothes before she spoke to anyone at all.

"Oh, hello there," a voice somewhere behind her said as she reached the top. "You must be the guest from America?"

Camille turned, smiled at the petite woman at the foot of the stairs. "And you must be Amanda," she said. "I've been meaning to come across to say hello."

Amanda Champagne, dressed in shorts and a big *I Love Jamaica* T-shirt, nodded and returned the smile. "Summer and Gavin aren't here. They've gone to take the cousins to the university. All of them, thank goodness. They're spending a semester here." She rolled her eyes. "Anyway, they asked me to let you know. And to help you get whatever you might need."

Camille pulled the top away from her body and wrinkled her nose. "I just really need a shower . . . and a change of clothes."

Amanda laughed. "OK. Go ahead then. Have you had breakfast, by the way? Mrs. Carydice has gone to the market, but she made pancakes this morning."

"Pancakes with bacon and syrup? I could really go for that." After a long night of hearty lovemaking, she was understandably famished.

Amanda nodded. "I'll get everything ready for you while you shower."

Half an hour later, Camille was bathed, perfumed, and dressed. This time in matching blue designer shorts and top with sky blue flip-flops. Amanda was busy in the kitchen when Camille knocked lightly on the door and said, "Here I am again, all refreshed."

Amanda beckoned her with a hand. "Come in and sit while I finish up the bacon."

Camille glanced at her watch and thought of

Harry. The poor thing would be starving, too. "Do you mind if I invite Harry in?"

Amanda paused in midstir. "Harry? Harry Britton?"

Camille nodded. "He's somewhere outside."

Amanda laid another few pieces of bacon in the pan. "He's probably over at the front house by now raiding the fridge bare. I wouldn't worry too much about him."

Camille propped her hand beneath her chin and leaned on the beautifully tiled counter.

"You sound as though you don't like him very much," Camille prodded gently. This was her chance to find out a few things about Mr. Harry Britton. He couldn't possibly be a wastrel through and through. Could he?

Amanda shrugged. "Harry is Harry. You know what I mean?"

Camille had no idea at all what she meant. "You mean he's irresponsible? And . . . generally . . ."

"He's a bum," Amanda said matter-of-factly. "A good-for-nothing slug." She lifted out several slices of bacon, rested them on a plate, then went across to a silver dome.

Camille nodded. It was just as she had thought.

Amanda lifted the dome. "How many pancakes? Two? Three?"

"Just two, please." She was anxious to get back to the discussion about Harry but didn't want to seem overly interested.

Amanda handed her the plate and came to sit opposite her on a stool.

"Do you know," Amanda said as soon as Camille began to tuck into the meal, "that he took my husband . . . *my husband* to a filthy girlie party at one of these hotels?"

Camille swallowed an entire hunk of pancake. "Really?" she croaked.

Amanda patted her on the back. "Yes, really. My husband, Nicholas . . . you've met him?"

Camille nodded.

"Anyway," Amanda continued. "Nicholas came home stinking to high heavens of smoke and booze, and God knows what else. And he had the nerve to tell me that nothing had happened. That it was all just innocent." She laughed in a brittle way. "An innocent boys' night out. But I know what happens whenever those two have any kind of a night out. Harry is a straight-out dog. And Nicky is a reformed one, with one foot right on the edge."

Camille chewed and considered how to handle this. She didn't want to make an enemy of Amanda Champagne, but at the same time, since she had been there at the filthy girlie party, she had a much better idea of what had gone on there. And Nicholas had not left with anyone.

Her brow furrowed in thought. As a matter of fact, he had stood against a wall for most of the time, with a drink in one hand. Totally alone.

"Well, I don't know Nicholas—your husband

very well, but from what little I was able to pick up, he seemed to me like a very settled family man. Many men develop that look, you know . . . when they stop chasing. And he has that look."

Amanda made a clicking sound with her tongue. "I wish I could believe that. But you don't know what he was like before I met him." She lifted Camille's glass, poured some juice. "I guess Summer would've told you already. Or maybe you guessed it. But I'm not Amber's mother."

Camille placed another forkful of pancake and bacon in her mouth. She had guessed that, since the child referred to Amanda by her first name. But what did that have to do with anything? "He was married before, then?"

Amanda laughed. "Nicky? Married before? No. Not him. He and that . . . that . . . Harry were both rakehells, you know? Girls, girls, girls. Partying every night. Never the same woman twice. And," she shrugged, "when you live like that, the lifestyle catches up with you sooner or later."

"So, that's how Amber came along."

Amanda nodded. "Pretty much. I mean, there's a whole long story behind that, but Amber's mother, after she had her, decided that she didn't want to raise her. So, of course, Nicky took the child away."

"He's a good man," Camille said, and she reached out to press Amanda's hand. "Truly. I can see it in him. How many men do you think, in the same situation, would actually step forward and raise a child born outside of wedlock?"

Amanda sighed. "I know that. And Amber's a sweet child. But . . ."

"You don't trust Nicholas, is that it?"

Amanda looked away, and when she turned her head again, she looked suspiciously close to tears. "I want to trust him. I really do. But he's so damn good-looking. Haven't you noticed? And trust me, women just fling themselves at him all the time. That's the trouble with marrying drop-dead gorgeous men. Every woman and her sister want them."

Camille finished the juice and poured herself a glass of water. The woman who married Harry Britton would have a similar problem, that was certain.

"Well, that's something you just have to deal with. Because unless he gets plastic surgery or something like that, that face is not gonna change. What I think you have to do, though, is trust him. If you don't . . ." She spread her fingers.

Amanda collected her plate, stood, and went to the sink. "I really just wish Harry would go back to Guyana. Things would be much better between Nicky and me if he wasn't constantly around, reminding Nicky of how things used to be."

Camille's eyebrows lifted a bit. "Guyana?" She'd had a feeling that Harry wasn't Jamaican. His accent was slightly different. More clipped in places.

"Harry's Guyanese." Amanda turned to look at her. "I guess you didn't know that?"

Camille stumbled into speech. "Oh, I don't really know that much about him at all. We've only just met." Well, not exactly, but how could she possibly explain that?

"Well, stay away from him if you have any interest in getting married. Because, trust me, he won't."

"Believe me, Harry's the last man on earth I'd ever marry. He's just not my . . . kind of guy." Her kind would have, at the barest minimum, a decent house to live in, a high-six-figure income, and a good car.

Amanda washed the plate and glass, put them to dry in the rack, and turned off the water. "Well, good for you."

Camille smiled. She'd wanted to ask more questions about Harry, but somehow the conversation had been sidetracked to Nicholas. But at least she had found out a few things about Harry. She now knew that he was from another country entirely. That he was most definitely a wastrel. And that Amanda Champagne couldn't stand him. Probably with very good reason.

The large wall clock in the living room donged on the half hour, and Camille glanced at her watch and gasped. Where had the time gone? "Shoot," she said. "It's eleven thirty. I've gotta get going. . . ." She paused. "Unless I can help you with anything?"

Amanda waved her suggestion away. "Forget it. There's nothing for you to do anyway."

The two women smiled at each other, and Camille said, "We'll have to talk again later."

Chapter Nineteen

Harry was waiting for her outside when she opened the door and trotted down the stairs.

"Why didn't you come in?" she asked.

He scratched an eyebrow. "Amanda's not very happy with me at the moment. So, I thought it might be best to stay out of the line of fire."

"Well, can you blame her? Taking her husband to a filthy girlie party, as she described it?"

Camille slung a leg over the leather seat, held on to him with a hand to steady herself, and then strapped the helmet on again.

"Need I remind you that you were at that filthy dirty party, missy?" He started the bike. "Anyway, you're right; she's right. I shouldn't have convinced Nick to go. I was wrong. Happy?"

"It's not me you've got to apologize to. I think you should buy her something. An 'I'm sorry' gift of some sort."

"Yeah," he grunted.

Camille clung to him as he stepped on the gas

and the bike surged off down the drive. For a minute she had forgotten who he was. Of course he wouldn't be able to afford a gift. Maybe she'd buy it for him. Amanda would never know the difference. Not unless he told her, of course. And why would he do a damn fool thing like that?

They shot down the coast road with Camille clinging to his back. The muscles in his shoulders rippled and pulled beneath her cheek, and she rested her head against the warmth of his back and closed her eyes. Although they were hurtling along at forty miles an hour or thereabouts, she felt safe with him.

"We'll stop at the market first, OK?"

Camille opened an eye. They were so close to the ocean now that the spray of each wave dotted her face with water. "The market?" she hollered against the wind.

"Open-air," he shot back. "They sell all sorts of things there."

"OK." It was fine with her. This was a side of Jamaica she had never seen before. A side that tourists who never left the luxury of their all-inclusive resorts never saw. But she was open to new experiences. She might even be able to pick up a few things for Lola. . . .

Camille's thoughts changed direction. She hadn't even called her friend since she had arrived on the island. Hadn't thought of her at all, if the truth be known. Hadn't thought of Anthony in the last twenty-four hours, either. It was all because of

Harry of course. He seemed to have the ability to make her forget about everything. He crooked his little finger at her, and she just jumped. That wasn't good. Wasn't good at all. After this little outing to Ocho Rios, she had to put some distance between them. She had to find another man to spend time with. Otherwise . . . otherwise she might end up wanting something more from the wastrel. And that wouldn't do anybody any good.

The road weaved away from the coastline and went inland for a bit. Thick trees with scaly branches overhung the road in certain spots, and every so often a half-naked child appeared on the side of the road, holding up a bunch of fruit. Harry waved a hand in salute at the smiling faces but didn't stop.

In a few more minutes, she and Harry were in the thick of traffic heading into Ocho Rios. He darted around trucks and cars of every make and description and continued to weave his way into the little town.

"It always gets crowded like this around lunchtime," he shouted. "You get around much faster if you're on a bike."

"Uhmm," Camille agreed, and squeezed her legs closer to the sides of the motorcycle. They were so close to any of a number of speeding cars that if anyone at all had had a touch too much to drink over brunch, Camille would surely lose a limb.

"We're nearly there."

Camille nodded and closed her eyes again. She wouldn't think about them hitting a bump in the road and catapulting right into the face of an on-coming truck. Harry knew what he was doing. Didn't he?

She opened an eye and stared right into the face of an older man seated at the wheel of a Mercedes-Benz convertible. She averted her gaze immedi-ately. She wanted no more men over fifty. As far as she was concerned, any man who was still unmar-ried at that age was either on the down low or prob-ably some sort of psychotic lunatic who no woman wanted any part of.

They were in the town now and Harry slowed the bike. Camille looked about her with interest. It was a densely built town with small, medium-sized, and large buildings pressed close together.

"There's been a lot of building done in the last ten years or so. Lots of new businesses have opened up shop."

"Look at that." Camille pointed to the colorfully painted sign hanging over what appeared to be an eatery of some sort. "Margaritaville. Remember that song by Jimmy Buffett?"

"Yeah," Harry said. "It's probably owned by an expatriate. You can always tell what's locally owned and what's not."

Camille wiped a hand under her chin. Without the rush of the wind in her face, the sun was suddenly scorching hot.

"You OK back there?"

"It's getting kinda hot. Pity these bikes don't come with air-conditioning."

Harry chuckled. "OK, softie. I'll get you out of the sun in just a minute."

They rode down a side street, stopped to let a huge crowd of tourists cross the road, cut through an alley and another street, until finally, sprawled before them was the market. There were rows and rows of wooden stands with fruits, vegetables, spices, dried salted fish, water coconuts, and sundry other items, and each stand was manned for the most part by women.

"Wow, is this it?" Camille asked, and there was a trace of bemusement in her voice.

Harry nodded. "This is it. I've gotta find a spot for my bike first, then we can go in and explore. Most of the really interesting stuff is deep inside. Usually, the fruits and vegetables are sold out here. But the clothes, trinkets, other stuff, are inside . . . underneath that roof over there."

He pointed to a large overhanging roof, and Camille asked with a slightly fearful note in her voice, "is it safe to go in there? It looks kinda dark."

"It's safe. Don't worry. Besides, you're with me, so what could happen to you?"

A smile curved the corners of her lips. "So, you're a brawler, huh? Somehow you don't look the type who would just break out and start throwing punches left and right if someone said some mess to your woman. You seem more like the pretty-boy type." And she made her voice squeaky. "You know, a lover, not a fighter."

Harry laughed. "Well, just goes to show you how wrong you can be about a person. I've been in my share of fights, in my younger years. My dad—" And he stopped.

"Your dad . . . what?"

Harry scooted the motorcycle into a rusty bicycle stand. "OK. You can get off. I'll just chain it to this. Should be safe here. Hey, man," he said to a passing vendor. "Watch my bike for me?"

The vendor came over. "Buy some of meh gennips and meh will watch you bike, bredda."

Harry grinned. "How you selling them?"

"Dem cheap, man," the man assured Harry with the consummate skill of a seasoned salesman. "And dem sweet, too. But prob'ly not as sweet as yuh wife, eh?" And he winked at Camille.

"Definitely not as sweet as me," she agreed, and she returned the man's wink and gave him a huge gamine grin.

"All right. All right," Harry agreed. "I'll buy some gennips, and you watch the bike. But leave my girl alone." And he tapped fists with the man.

"All right, boss."

Camille stood back watching the exchange. Harry had called her his girl. Now why had he done that? She wasn't his girl and couldn't ever be his girl, either. But there was no point in bringing that up now. It would soon be crystal clear to him that she was not his exclusive property.

He stretched his hand for hers once he was through chaining the bike.

"What were you saying about your dad?" she asked him now.

"My dad?" His brow furrowed; then he said, "Oh, right. It's not important."

"Hmm," she said. "He probably wanted you to get a job, right? Make something of yourself? Stop bumming around, wasting your life?"

"Close. Close," he said, and then pointed her attention toward the vendor who had agreed to watch the bike. "Let's go across and get the fruits before he thinks we're trying to run off without them. Ever tasted gennips before?"

They spent two hours walking leisurely around the market, sampling all kinds of wonderful fruit. Drinking coconut water directly from the nut. Picking through strings of blue and white coral bracelets. Munching on piping hot beef patties. And generally having a good time. Harry joked good-naturedly with the male vendors and warned them off with the same good humor when they got too fresh with Camille.

In the end, Camille bought an ankle-length sundress for herself and a *Smile Jamaica* hat for Harry. He accepted it with a quizzical look and an exaggerated, "For me?"

Camille grinned at his expression, wagged a finger at him, and said, "Don't give this gift away, either."

"Don't worry; I'll be keeping this," he promised, and he slung an arm about her shoulders and pressed a warm kiss to the side of her face.

They meandered through the rest of the afternoon in this manner. Laughing. Talking. Laughing some more. Until the pressing afternoon heat had faded to a breezy warmth. Camille walked back to the motor-bike with glowing eyes. This simple outing, which had probably cost thirty U.S. dollars tops, had been so much fun. In fact, she couldn't remember the last time when she had had such an enjoyable day.

"You know," and she held on to the fingers of the hand that was draped over her shoulder, "I'd always thought that you needed a lot of money to have a good time. But you don't."

She looked into his silky black eyes, but the expression there was unreadable.

"And I thought you didn't have any money at all?" Yet he had bought just about everything they had eaten. Maybe he was just a good saver. Or maybe he hadn't given away that chain after all.

Harry's eyebrows lifted. "Did I say that?"

"No, but . . ."

He touched the tip of her nose with a finger. "Let's forget about money for a little while, deal?"

She nodded. "Deal."

They spent the remainder of the afternoon at Dunns River Falls, and Camille climbed all the way to the top of the gushing water, balancing herself on big slippery boulders and shrieking with laughter whenever a rush of water knocked Harry off his feet.

"One thing you're not so good at, huh?" she called to him from the top.

"You're a wicked woman, Camille Roberts," Harry said in response. And Camille tossed handfuls of water at him until he finally made it to the rock where she sat.

He hauled himself out of the water and flopped backward on the boulder, his skin smooth and gleaming in the fading light.

Camille played with his hair and looked down at the rushing river of white water as it fell and rolled its way down the rocky incline and out to blend with the ocean. It was wonderful. Magical. And to think that she had lived this long and yet she had never had a day that felt so special. So very sweet. Maybe there was more to life than all of the material things that money could buy. Maybe the really important things were . . . right here.

She looked at Harry, lying there with his eyes closed, and her fingers stopped playing with his hair. Lord Almighty, what was she saying? She must have sunstroke or something. After just two days of being with him, she was ready to abandon all of her plans of wealth and privilege to become a . . . a layabout like him? God, she was out of her mind.

She shifted away from him on the rock, and he opened his eyes to stare at her.

"Isn't this beautiful?" And he took the flat of her

palm and rubbed it against his chest. A ripple of sensation caught Camille by surprise, and she blinked and said a startled, "Oh."

He kissed the heart of her palm. "Feeling OK?"

Camille nodded. For some reason, her heart had begun to pump hard and heavy in her breast, and for a full minute she didn't trust herself to speak. When she was in control again, she said with a trace of regret in her voice, "I think we should go. It's beginning to get dark."

Camille shaded her eyes and looked out at the red sunset. It *was* beautiful. The sky was an artist's canvas filled with pinks, oranges, golds, all streaking wonderfully together.

She sucked in a deep breath and let it back out. Now she knew what it meant to truly exhale. Peace had come to her in the most sudden and unexpected way. But what did it all mean?

Harry watched the play of emotions across her face and felt a moment of sympathy. Maybe Gavin and Summer had been right to warn him off of playing this game with her. But he hadn't expected her to be this soft inside. It really bothered him that she was this soft inside. He had wanted her to be a hard-as-nails kind of woman. The kind who would benefit well from what he intended to teach her. The kind he could walk away from without a backward glance. But she wasn't hard. She wasn't hard at all.

"We're not going to sleep here, are we?" She was looking at him now with questioning eyes that were slightly wet around the edges and he suddenly felt like holding her. Holding her and soothing all of her pain away. Jesus, he was getting soft.

"Let's go then," he said with a gruff note in his voice.

They rode back to Champagne Cove with the night just behind them. And by the time they had turned onto the property, the darkness had caught them. Harry crunched up the gravel drive, past the front house, and then on to the manor house, which stood a good distance behind. Camille got off the bike, undid the helmet, and handed it back to him.

"So . . ." he said, and he leaned forward to rest on the handles of the motorcycle.

Camille chewed on a corner of her lip. She had to let him know that she wouldn't be coming to see him again. That this thing between them had been just that. A thing. She wasn't his girl. Couldn't ever be his girl.

She swallowed. "Harry . . . I want you to know that I . . . I mean, that I've never had a nicer, more perfect day than the one I had today." She felt her throat go thick and strangled, and paused to clear it. "What I'm trying to say, and am making a mess of, is that I had a really, really good time."

He looked at her with steady eyes and said, "I sense that there's a 'but' in there somewhere."

Camille sighed. There were so many "buts" in there that if she tried to explain them all she and Harry would be there all night long.

"This thing between us . . ." she gestured with a hand, "is good, but it's not going to work out."

"Why not?"

"Why not?" What did he mean, "Why not?" Surely she didn't need to . . . to spell the whole thing out? Did he really think that she was the kind of woman who would be content living in a shack, for God's sake? Did he for one solitary minute really think that?

"We come from different worlds," she tried again. "And I'm not the kind of woman who can just be with a man for . . . for the physical thing. You know what I mean?" She held up a hand as he drew breath to speak. "I know what you're going to say. 'What about the whole thing at Hedonism?' But that was different. I was getting married, and it was just one last indulgence. But things are different now. I'm getting older, do you see?"

He shifted his lean a bit and asked in a calm and completely unperturbed manner, "Getting older than what?"

Camille brought her lips together. "What do you mean, older than what?" He knew exactly what she was trying to say but was bent on being completely obtuse. "I'm thirty-six years old. That's right. Thirty-six. And I can't afford to waste any time on something that's going nowhere. I want to get married. Have a life. A family. Just like every other woman. And you . . ."

"Ah." He sat up straight. "And you think that I'm not marriage material. Is that it?"

That wasn't it. Maybe he could be marriage material for another kind of woman but just not for her. Why couldn't he get what she was trying to tell him? Why did he want her to come out and say it? He was poor. Poor. Poor. Poor. And she couldn't deal with that kind of life. Living in a shack by the sea. Depending on the charity of others. Finally growing to hate him because he had completely ruined all of her chances at a smooth and easy life. She didn't want that. And if he knew her, really knew her, he wouldn't want that, either.

"You . . . we're just not right for each other. So, I don't think there's any point in trying to . . ."

"Why aren't we 'right for each other,' as you say?"

Camille shifted from one foot to the next. He was going to force it out of her. He was going to make her say it. She took a breath to clear her head. OK. Fine. He wanted her to say it, so she would say it.

"You have no money. OK? And I only date men who have money." There, she had said it. She was sorry to have done it in such a bald and cold manner, but he had forced it from her. Now he would go away and leave her to her own plans.

Harry nodded, and a hard light came into his eyes. Yes. Now this was the kind of woman he had thought her to be. This was the kind of woman that he could handle. That he loved to handle.

He tapped a finger on the metal handle of the bike. "Money. Hmm. So, if I had some money, you're saying that things would be different. But since, as you say, I have none, you can't waste your time on me."

Camille folded her arms about her. Put like that, her attitude seemed cold, mean-spirited, shallow. But what was the point in beating around the bush? It was far better that he know it now than at some point down the road.

"I'm sorry," she said. "That's just the way it is for me. I can't live a struggling kind of life. It's just not in me to live that way."

Harry smiled, but the smile didn't quite reach his eyes. "So, that's it then, hmm?"

She stepped back from him. "That's it."

He adjusted the fit of his helmet. "Sure you won't change your mind?"

"I won't change my mind."

"Not even for a little sex?"

Camille sighed. That was exactly how this whole thing got started. "Not even for that."

Chapter Twenty

Camille let herself in the front door of the house feeling twisted and wretched. He had said good-bye to her very nicely and then had just ridden off. Not a backward look, not a hug, not a last kiss of farewell. Nothing. But what could she expect really? She had told the man that she didn't want anything more to do with him after they had spent a wonderful two days together. And not because he had treated her badly or done some other terrible thing. Just because he was without funds or ambition.

She closed the door behind her and locked it. She was a horrible person. She was just beginning to realize it now. Maybe that was the reason God had sent a man like Anthony Davis into her life. Damn it. But what was she supposed to do?

Camille heard the sound of dinnerware clinking and darted quickly up the stairs. She just couldn't face anyone at all right then. She needed to think, all alone and by herself. If Harry had berated her, attacked her in some way, her mind would have closed down and she would have gotten all tight and defensive. But he hadn't done that. He'd just looked at her in that certain kind of way that had made her feel so very small. So very cheap.

She pushed the bedroom door open and entered. The room was immaculate. The bedsheets had been changed; her shoes, which she had discarded earlier in the day, were positioned neatly by the foot of the bed. And the veranda door was thrown open so that fresh sea air rolled gently through.

She sat on the edge of the bed to remove her flip-flops, then went to the bathroom. A hot shower would make everything seem much better.

Forty-five minutes later, Camille emerged from the bathroom wrapped in a soft white terry robe. She ran a towel down her wet streaming hair, shuffled her feet into a pair of bedroom slippers, and then went to stand on the veranda. Her eyes drifted down the beach and she squinted for a second at a lone figure standing at the water's edge. She couldn't quite make out who it was, but it appeared to be a man.

She pressed her face into the freshly laundered towel. She knew who it was of course. It was Harry, wading about in the water, trying to catch his evening meal. She sniffled. Poor thing. He had quite probably spent every last dime he possessed on her today. And what had she done as a way of saying thank you? She had insulted him. Insulted him.

She turned to go back in and almost tripped over a little body standing directly behind her.

"Adam," she said, genuinely startled. "Have you been standing there all along?" She'd been so wrapped up in her thoughts that she hadn't even heard him come in.

"Auntie," he said with a sweet note in his voice. "Can you read me a bedtime 'tory?"

Camille looked down at him, and the tight feeling in her chest receded by just a bit. Children were such joys. They made everything seem on, somehow.

"Sure, honey," she said, and she bent to lift him into her arms. "Have you brought any books with you?"

He nodded and pointed at the bed. "I brought my fav'rite one. It has lots of good 'tories. Especially for when you're sad. Are you sad, Auntie?" And he looked into her face with steady golden eyes.

Camille blinked rapidly. Now how had he known that? She put him in the middle of the bed and sat beside him. "Does Mummy know where you are?"

The little head nodded. "She said I could ask you."

Camille ruffled the curls on his head. "Sure?"

"Sure." And he beamed at her.

"OK then. One story and then I take you back to Mummy and Daddy." She picked up the thick book of fairy tales and thumbed through it.

Adam stopped the flow of pages with a finger after a moment and said, "This one, Auntie. This one."

Camille settled herself more comfortably on the bed and began to read about mischievous squirrels and naughty bunnies. A few minutes into the tale, Adam's head lolled heavily against her shoulder, and he asked in a very sleepy voice, "Auntie, can foxes really talk?"

Camille paused in the telling of the tale, not exactly sure how to answer that one. She didn't want to ruin the story for the darling little thing.

"Well, if you believe—" But what she was saying was interrupted by the gentle puffs of his breath against her arm. She looked at him for long minutes, just watching the rise and fall of his chest. The movement of his eyes beneath his eyelids. Everything was so simple when you were a child. So very simple. If only life for adults could be the same way.

She went across to the bathroom mirror, braided her hair into a thick plait, and then slid into a loose-fitting T-shirt and a pair of jeans. When she was through, she lifted Adam into her arms, nestled his head beneath her chin, and went in search of Summer.

She knocked gently on what she knew was the master bedroom door, and when Summer's voice said, "Come," she entered.

"So, he found you again." Summer smiled. She was propped up in bed against two huge pillows, reading.

Camille returned her smile. "He wanted a bedtime story, but he fell asleep right in the middle of it."

Summer closed the book. "He'd been asking for you all day. 'Where's Auntie? Where's Auntie?' Finally I had to tell him that you were with Uncle Harry." She laughed. "The boy is totally in love with you."

Camille's heart thumped. What boy? "Harry?" she asked with a little squeak in her voice.

Summer took Adam from her and said, "Maybe Harry, too."

Camille grinned foolishly. "Do you really think so?"

Summer walked through the master to a connecting bedroom, placed Adam gently in bed, rolled the covers up beneath his chin, and kissed him on a flushed cheek.

She walked back through to where Camille was still standing. "Do you have a minute?" she asked.

Camille followed her out onto a very spacious veranda and sat in a softly cushioned lounge chair facing the ocean. Summer pulled up a similar chair and stretched out on it with one leg bent.

"I sometimes sit out here at night and just enjoy the breeze. It's great, isn't it?"

"Umm," Camille agreed. "You have an absolutely lovely house. And an absolutely lovely family." She sighed. "You have it all, really."

Summer said nothing for a long moment. Then she asked, "Is this what you want?"

Camille was startled. "What do you mean?"

"I mean, the house, the cars, the . . . money?"

And at Camille's troubled look she added, "I hope you don't mind me asking you that?"

"No. It's OK. Really." Camille found the words thick and heavy on her tongue. Had her little conversation with Harry been overheard? What must Summer think of her now?

Summer opened a tin of chocolate shortbread cookies that sat on the round table between them and offered it to her. When they were both crunching on the delicious sweets, Summer continued, "You know, I used to think that material things were all-important. And I almost married the wrong man because of it. Remember, I told you that?"

Camille took another cookie and crunched on it. She vaguely remembered Summer mentioning something about almost marrying some other guy.

"Kevin?" Camille asked.

Summer nodded and poured them each a glass of ice-cold water. "You see," she said, leaning forward, "I really think the way the universe works is . . . well, if you go after something with the wrong motives in your heart, you might end up getting that thing you're chasing, but in most cases, it'll turn out to be much, much less than what you actually should have gotten had your motives been pure."

Camille was silent for a long moment. Maybe Summer was right. She had almost ended up with Anthony. In fact, she would have ended up with Anthony had she not returned home that day just two hours early. She rubbed the corner of an eye and tried her best to hold the threatening tears at bay. "But," and she wiped at a spot beneath her right eye, "how do you get what you want, then? I mean, you have to know what you want, right? In order to get it? You have to set goals and then go for them. Isn't that what everybody always says?"

Summer leaned forward to squeeze her hand. "Setting goals is fine. In fact, you have to do it if you want to get ahead in life. But you have to set the right kind of goal. You can say, 'I'd like to become a doctor.' That's a good goal. And if you do the work, and put in the time, after a number of years, you can achieve that goal. But," and she stopped to get another cookie, "the kind of goal that hardly ever works out well is the kind that involves trapping someone, or using someone for material gain. Do you see what I mean?"

A tear spilled from Camille's left eye, and Summer reached into a pocket and then handed her a handkerchief. And Summer continued speaking, as though Camille weren't sobbing her eyes out right beside her.

"Take Harry for instance. He's a very laid-back kind of guy, and—"

"I know," Camille said between sobs. "He's a bum. A worthless good-for-nothing bum. Amanda already told me all about him."

Summer blinked. "She did? What did she say?"

Camille blew her nose, wiped the corner of each nostril. "Just that he'll never amount to anything, or something like that. And that he was a lazy slug. Not marriage material." She sniffled and blew her nose again. "I don't really remember what else she said. But that kind of sums everything up."

"Hmm," Summer said, and took a long drink of water. "Mandy's upset with him. That's why she said all that. Harry's really a nice guy. He's a little too much into the ladies, because they're constantly throwing themselves at him." She gave her stomach a rub. "I even had to send my cousin Francine off to the university a little early, to get her out of his hair. But he's truly a nice guy. A diamond in the rough, I think."

"But say you weren't married to Gavin, and didn't have all this." Camille swept her hand out in an arc. "Say you were like me. No money to speak of. No job. Would you even date him?"

Summer scraped her hair back behind both ears. "Would I date Harry?"

Camille nodded. "Uhm-hmm. Would you?"

"If I liked him, I would. If I was attracted to him, I would. And if I didn't have money," she shrugged, "I'd get myself a job. Why should a man have to pay my way through life? I just couldn't live with myself if I ever came to that."

Camille absorbed that in silence. Maybe Summer was right. Lola had said almost the same thing, too.

Camille's forehead wrinkled. How had she become this person? This clinging, dependent gold digger? She wasn't really that way. She had never been that way when she was younger. What had happened to her along the way? She had to think. She had to think.

Summer rubbed her stomach again. "God, these cookies are riding up on me in the worst way."

Camille stood. "You're pregnant. That's why."

"No. I'm really not," Summer shook her head. "The test was negative."

"A home test?"

"Yep."

Camille bent to give Summer a hug. "Well, do it again. I'm going to go off to bed now."

"Think about what I said, though," Summer called to her as she walked back through the bedroom.

Camille nodded. She would think about it. She would.

Chapter Twenty-one

The next two weeks flew by. August was hot and full of bristle and greenery. Sunday dinners were had at either Summer and Gavin's house or Nicky and Amanda's. And Camille was happy to see that Amanda was getting along much better now with her husband. Camille had even surprised them one day cuddling in the kitchen. She hadn't asked Summer any questions about what had brought about the change in Amanda but wondered from time to time whether or not her shift in attitude had been due to the little talk they had had. It was a fond little thought that she played with from time to time, that she, Camille Roberts, could have somehow managed to influence some part of the wonderful Champagne family. So she hung on to it on the days when she stared out at the sea, feeling the breeze, seeing the blue, but still feeling empty and achy inside. She tried her best not to think of Harry, but every night before she went to bed, thoughts of him would sneak in between the covers and lie there with her. And she would stay awake for hours, just thinking. Thinking. Summer was right. It was one of the universal laws of nature. If anyone approached any objective at all with impure motives, the outcome of all of that would also be impure. Why hadn't she realized that? She had wasted so many years in hot pursuit of exactly nothing.

Almost two weeks to the day after she had so rudely insulted Harry, she decided to make amends. She had spent many nights turning over and over in her mind how to do exactly this, and one morning, after praying about it for half the night, she had woken up and known exactly what she should do. She would apologize to him. She would tell him that she'd been wrong. She would beg him to forgive her, and then she would flourish her trump card. Her ace. Her surefire winner.

Camille stood on the sand outside the little shack now and decided to try a session of hollering first. She cupped her mouth and screamed his name. Once. Twice. A third time. Her voice rose in the air and then spread out on the wind. Maybe he wasn't at home? Or maybe he'd heard her but decided not to answer.

She nodded to no one in particular. That was probably closer to the truth of it. He most likely didn't want to speak to her again. And who could blame him?

She walked over to the rope that was slung up the

cliff side, yanked at it to test its strength, and then placed her foot on the first carved-out step. The climb took her less than five minutes, and once she'd gotten to the top of the slope she bent over a bit to get her breath back. Then marched right across to the front door and up the rickety stairs to knock. She might be a terrible person when it came right down to it, but she was no coward. She would face him. And, if possible, she would win him back.

She pounded on the wood, listened, and then pounded again. After a few knocks, she heard the sound of footsteps. Her heart pounded in her chest. What if he chased her off his property? What if he slammed the door in her face? What if—

The door opened, and there he stood, dressed in a faded red T-shirt and blue jeans. His eyes were steady, his face completely blank. "Yes?"

Camille swallowed away the anxious spot of dryness in her throat. She tried a smile but found that her lips wouldn't stretch in a way that seemed natural. Well, she would just jump in then. She would just say what she came to say and feel the punishment of his tongue if he decided that was what she deserved. She was ready for anything. "I came over to see you."

He folded his arms and didn't step away from the mouth of the door to invite her in. "And?"

She gritted her teeth. OK. She could deal with this. "I wanted to tell you . . . to explain how sorry I am for all of the things I said to you two weeks ago."

His brows lifted. "Really?"

"Yes. Really. I was wrong. Stupid. Unkind. Stop me anytime you like," she tried a little joke.

He didn't smile at her. "And what has caused this reversal in attitude? This sudden revelation?"

"I know I deserve all of this," she said, "but can I come in? The sun's hot, and I have something else I want to talk over with you."

"Are you sure my house isn't too poor for you?"

Camille's temper increased by just a tick. "I told you I was sorry for all that."

"And you expect me to just forgive you and welcome you back? Is that it? Just like that."

"It would be nice if you did. But I'm not expecting too much."

He turned away from the door, and Camille closed her eyes. He was going to slam the door in her face. Oh God.

"Come in," he said as he walked back into the belly of the house.

Camille followed him, her eyes sweeping left and right. "You bought some chairs," she said, and there was a happy note in her voice. That was an improvement, surely.

"I picked them up at a flea market sale. Very cheap. I haven't had a chance to really check them out yet, so I can't vouch for their cleanliness."

"No," she assured him quickly, "they look good." And they did, if you ignored the fact that they appeared a little frayed around the edges.

She sat and crossed her legs. She had purposely worn a very short pair of shorts and hoped that he would notice the smooth length of her legs.

He sat, too, leaning forward to rest his arms on his thighs. When she said nothing immediately, he prompted her with, "So what was this thing that you wanted to talk to me about?"

"Well, I know you won't believe this . . . won't even really understand what it's taken to get me here. But here goes. For years, most of my adult life, actually, I've always wanted to be rich, you know? To have a really comfortable, luxurious kind of life. So, I chased after men for the money. And I've always had it dead set in my mind that I would marry a wealthy guy. Anyway," and she waved a hand to indicate that that was all over with now, "I've done a lot of thinking. A lot of thinking. And I understand now about the importance of motive and—"

Harry's eyebrows flicked upward. "Motive?"

She looked down at her legs, back up at him. "It's a long story; trust me. But the important thing is I was confused, you see. About . . . about everything. But I did some praying about it, too, and things are clearer to me now."

Harry sat back. He hadn't expected this to happen so very soon. When Summer had called him to let him know that Camille was on the way over, he had had to hurry through his conference call with the office. He hadn't known what she might be up to now. He knew that she was a highly sexed woman, though, so naturally, he had assumed that after a couple of weeks of forced celibacy on her part, she had decided to come over again to tempt him with a little of the delicious. He had known that she would come to him eventually, of course. So, he had just dug in his heels and waited her out. But instead of her demanding sex and possibly wrestling him to the floor, she was rambling on about motives and prayer and . . . what?

He rubbed an index finger against the side of his head. "What was that?"

Camille repeated herself again. This time with slow and deliberate intent. "I said that I'm going to get myself a job. And I want you to agree to do the same thing." She fished around in her pocket and removed a scrap of newsprint. "I found a job for a headwaiter, maître d' type, over at the Sans Souci resort. It would be perfect for you. Look." And she handed over the paper and sat back with a bright, expectant look.

Harry looked down at the scrap of paper. "A maître d' at the Sans?" He kept his face tight and expressionless. "They wouldn't hire me for that," he said after a minute of struggling to maintain his composure.

Camille leaned forward. "But they would. You're exactly what they're looking for. You're well-spoken. Good-looking. Charming. Intelligent. Good with people. Why wouldn't they hire you?"

"Because I have zero experience in the hotel or

food business." And if he turned up there looking for a job, the owner, whose legal affairs Harry handled routinely, might keel over with a coronary.

"Harry," Camille tried again, "you can't continue living like this. Don't you understand? You've never told me your age, but I'd guess you're around thirty-five or -six? Right?"

He cleared his throat. "Thirty-eight, actually."

She nodded. "Thirty-eight then. Even worse." She took a breath and plowed on. "You've got to start making provisions for your old age, even if you don't get married. I mean, you don't want to be a toothless old man wandering around on the beach looking for fish and grubs."

This time Harry laughed. "Fish and grubs?"

She waved the comment away. "You know what I mean. You can live this way when you're young. But God help you if old age finds you exactly here, in the same place, in the same situation. I don't want that to happen to you. I don't want that to happen to me."

He gave her a glinting look. "But you're going to marry a rich man, so why should you even worry about all of that?"

She hung her head and gave him a woebegone look. "I'm not going to marry a rich man. I may not even marry any kind of man at all."

He rested his chin on steepled fingers. "So, how do you intend to live?"

She frowned at him. "Haven't you been listening to a single word I've said? I'm going to get a job.

I'm not really that qualified for anything, but Summer's offered to help me find something in PR. And once I save enough money, I plan to open a restaurant called Camille's Kitchen. But, and here's the catch, I'm not going to do it unless you do it, too."

Harry gave her a startled look. "Unless I do what, too?"

"Unless we both get jobs. Me a job. You a job."

Harry's eyes met hers. She had balls, this girl. *This woman.* But she had heart, too. Imagine setting forth a stipulation like that. She would only work if he did.

"I'm not going to get a job."

She crossed and uncrossed her legs, and Harry's eyes followed the movement.

"Come on, Harry. Don't you want to really fix this place up? Clean up the outside? Put in a nice bathroom with a bathtub and an inside toilet?" He liked hot water, for goodness' sake. Could nothing motivate him at all?

He shrugged. "I'll do it in my own way. In my own time."

Camille massaged her temples. Well, she had tried. And if she was completely honest, she would have to admit that she hadn't really expected him to go for the idea at all. It had been unrealistic of her to think that he would just jump at the chance to work. Maybe there was some deep-rooted psychological reason that he wouldn't. Or maybe he didn't think that she was serious about working herself. Or maybe he was just a good-for-nothing bum. God in heaven, why had she fallen in love with *him?* Was this to be her punishment because she had lived for so many years with impure motives?

She sucked in a breath and covered her mouth. The whole complexity of the situation had just hit her. She did love him. She hadn't realized it until this very minute. Until the thought had articulated itself in her mind. Oh God, what a mess. But how could she love him, for goodness' sake? It was impossible. Unrealistic. Ridiculous.

He gave her a quizzical look. "What's the matter now?"

Camille shook her head. "Nothing. Nothing at all." And she gave him such a tortured look that his heart warmed to her.

Harry got up, walked across to a window, peered out at the ocean. He chewed on the corner of his lip as the thoughts coursed through his mind. He had no idea, no idea at all, why he would even consider doing anything this ridiculous, given everything. Maybe he was losing his mind. Maybe he'd been working too hard and now he was losing his freaking mind.

He turned back to her with hands stuffed into his pockets.

"You'll work if I work?"

Her eyes darted up to his. "Yes. I promise."

"You'll stand on your own two feet? Make your own money? No more relying on handouts from rich men? No more trying to marry rich men?"

She nodded with enthusiasm. "Yes, I told you that already. I truly believe now that this whole thing of me trying to marry a rich man was the reason why my life was so messed up. Summer really hit the nail on the head when we had our little talk."

"Summer convinced you of this?"

"She did."

Harry came to sit again. He would have to remember to thank Summer. The girl was not only beautiful and kindhearted; she was also a genius. She had managed to do in one session of conversation what he might not have been able to do in months of slowly breaking down Camille's need for material things.

"OK," he said after another stretch of thinking. "I'll do it."

Camille pressed her hands together. God be praised.

"You'll get yourself a job," she repeated just to be certain that they were both talking about the same thing.

"I'll get myself a job."

Camille bounded from her chair, and before Harry could even react, she was all over him, smothering him with kisses.

"Wait a minute. Wait a minute," he said after she had managed to kiss his entire face. "I still haven't forgiven you for what you said about me being dirt-poor."

"I'm sorry," Camille said, and she kissed him

again. "Forgive me? Please? I really am sorry I said all that. I didn't mean it. I was just scared, is all."

"Hmm," Harry said, and he leaned back and let her kiss him. Strangely, he was beginning to really like this woman. Maybe more than just like her. But he would stand on that feeling hard. He didn't really want her. And he had to remember that. He *had* to remember that.

"So, what job will you try to get?" Camille asked him. "The one I showed you in the paper?"

He gave her an innocent look. "How about a lawyer?"

Camille shoved at his shoulder. "Come on now. Be serious."

"OK," he agreed. "The one in the paper then. And if I can't get that one, I'll try for a waiter's job. Good?"

Camille nodded. Good. Very good. It wasn't the best job in the world, but it was a start.

Chapter Twenty-two

Summer bit worriedly on the corner of a nail. "Harry, this is going too far. We're already in too deep, and now this? How are you going to work as a waiter in Ocho Rios? Are you completely out of your mind? Everyone there knows you. And have you thought of this little bit of trivia? What if one of your clients walks into the place and catches you balancing a plate of fried mackerel and rice on your head? Have you thought of that?"

Harry finished adjusting his tie before the mirror and turned to give Summer a smile. "Don't worry about a thing. I have it well in hand. I'm going to do the worst interview a human being has ever done." He chuckled. "If they give me that job after I'm done with them, then they need to close up shop immediately. Don't worry," he said again. "I'm not going to get the job. I'm not going to get any of the jobs. But she will."

Summer took a turn about the room. "But how long are you going to keep this up, Harry? When she finds out who you really are, she's going to hate you. More important, she's going to hate me."

Harry brushed the sides of his hair. "I don't think she'll hate you. But she'll probably hate me. Which is for the best anyway."

"But you're in love with her."

Harry gave Summer a sharp look. "I am most definitely not in love with her."

Summer crossed her arms before her and gave him an unconvinced, "Umm-hmm. Then why are you going to all of this trouble? Have you thought of that? And don't give me the whole gold digger thing, either, because as many women as you've run into in your life, you must have met a few who were after you just for the money."

Harry put his finger to his lips and mouthed, *Ssh, she's coming.*

Camille clipped smartly up the stairs. She was dressed in a blue navy suit, her hair nicely pinned up. Gold earrings in her ears. She could have been a doctor, a lawyer, a Wall Street guru.

She knocked on the door, poked her head around. "All set?"

Harry came forward so that she could see him clearly. He was dressed in a pair of neatly pressed pinstriped pants, a whiter than white shirt, and a maroon tie.

"All set," he said. And he looked her over with an appreciative eye. "Now, if they don't hire you, then they need their heads examined."

Camille beamed. "You don't look too bad your-self."

Summer walked out onto the rickety front stairs, and Camille gave her a big hug.

"Thanks so much for lending us the Jeep. It's kind of hard to go to an interview on the back of a motorcycle."

Summer gave her a perturbed look and muttered, "That's OK."

A few minutes later, they were belted into their seats and Harry was leaning out the driver's window to say, "Wish me luck."

Summer watched them go with a shake of her head. This was definitely the craziest thing Harry Britton had ever done. And he had dragged her into the whole thing with him. But maybe it would work out for the best. Maybe he had finally found the right woman. Maybe.

On the road to Ocho Rios, Camille pulled out a little notebook and reviewed the notes she had jotted there. "Now remember," she said to Harry. "Don't give them too much information. Make sure you just answer what they ask you. And don't slouch in the chair. OK? Sit up straight and if they ask you if you've ever done this kind of work before, tell them you have. Make up something."

Harry smiled at her. She was so darned cute. "And do you have any dos and don'ts for your interview?"

"Uhm, I spoke to Lola last night about the whole

thing, and she told me that I should just be myself. Besides, I think Gavin put in a good word for me with the manager of the hotel, so I think I'll get the job. Even though my credentials are a little lacking."

"Hospitality director," Harry said. "I like the sound of that."

"Not director, you silly man. I'll just be a specialist. A hospitality specialist. If I get the job, that is. I'll walk around the hotel, meeting and greeting guests, you know, and generally making sure that they're having a good time."

They chatted for the remainder of the way about this and that until finally they were pulling up before the hotel. Camille took a deep breath. All of a sudden, she felt nervous. She flipped open the mirror section on the sun visor, fixed a stray hair.

"Do I look OK?"

Harry stroked the side of her face with a thumb. "You look good," he said. "Don't worry; you can do this. Remember Lola's advice. Don't pick your nose or anywhere else."

"Harry!" Camille exclaimed. But she laughed, too. "You're such an idiot."

He smiled and kissed her on the cheek. "Good luck. And I'll be waiting for you out here when you're all done."

He waved at her as she clipped smartly across the cobblestone parking lot. And she turned again to look at him when she got to the door. He sat back in his seat and closed his eyes once she had disappeared inside. Summer really didn't know what she was talking about. In love with Camille Roberts? Ridiculous.

He glanced at his watch. Almost two o'clock. He would make a few calls to the office to check on things, and then he would go in and do the world's worst interview.

Chapter Twenty-three

"I got it. I got it. I got it." Camille slammed into the Jeep with glowing eyes and a beatific smile on her face. "Can you imagine it? They hired me on the spot." She grinned at Harry. Other than what she experienced when having sex with him, this was one of the best feelings she had ever had in her life. It made her feel as though she had accomplished something.

"Congratulations. I knew you could do it." Harry gave her a hard hug and then kissed her flush on the lips. His interview had not gone nearly as well, of course.

"But what about you?" she asked now, her eyes still gleaming with excitement. "How did yours go?"

Harry started the engine. "Not so well."

Camille adjusted her skirt. "What do you mean, not so well?"

She waited for him to pull out onto the road and into traffic before prodding again, "What do you mean? Did they say something to you?"

Harry stroked a hand down his nose. They had in fact said quite a few things to him. And none of them had been at all complimentary. "They asked me to leave the premises actually."

Camille's mouth popped open. "They asked you to what?"

"Leave the premises."

She struggled for words. "What . . . I mean is, why? What happened?"

"You want to hear the whole sordid thing?"

She pressed his hand and gave him such a look of sympathy that Harry was flooded with waves of guilt. "Tell me."

Harry cleared his throat. "Well, I was sitting in this room, you know, waiting for the interviewer to come in. And he did say I should be there at about two fifteen or thereabouts."

She nodded, listening with rapt attention. "Aha."

"Well, he . . . the interviewer, Mr. Phillips, was a bit tardy, you see. So, I drifted off to sleep for a while. And it was kind of uncomfortable trying to catch a few winks in that straight-backed chair, so I took my shoes off, put my feet up on his desk, and got comfortable."

Camille covered her mouth with a hand. "Oh no."

"He woke me up, though. But he seemed so nice and concerned about me that I asked him if he would mind coming back in a half an hour or so. I was truly tired."

Camille gave him a horrified stare and an, "Oh God, no."

"Well, that perfectly reasonable question seemed to kind of set him off. He used a few choice phrases that I won't repeat, and then he told me that if I wasn't off the premises in five minutes flat, he'd make sure I was thrown off."

Camille looked at Harry's face, trying to ascertain if he was joking or not. "Are you serious? You really did that?"

He nodded. "Dead serious."

"But Harry," she began, "how could you think that you could just take a nap like that? Are you completely out of your mind? This was a job interview, for heaven's sake. Not a . . . a . . . Anyway." She massaged her forehead. "It's not the end of the world. You can interview for something else, somewhere else." She was beginning to suspect that he had done this deliberately just because he didn't want to work. Hell and damnation, but why was he so absolutely unambitious? It was unnatural.

"Let's go eat something to celebrate."

Camille stared at him. He didn't care at all. He wasn't even remotely upset about what had happened. God. What was she going to do? What was she going to do?

"Do you really feel like eating, now?"

Harry grinned at her in a completely unperturbed manner, and Camille felt like slapping him hard.

"Why not? You've gotten yourself a job, right? It's a great achievement. Besides, I'm hungry."

"But you didn't get yours."

He swung the Jeep into the Hot Pot II restaurant, cut the engine, and turned in his seat to face her. "I'll get something soon. I will. So don't look so upset about it."

Camille unbuckled the belt. "I'm more upset that you're not upset. Doesn't anything at all even faze you?"

"Come on," he said. "Let's not fight." And he opened the automatic doors and chatted to her all the way into the restaurant about how very good the food and wine were there. They were seated quickly, since they had arrived at an off-peak hour, and very soon a waiter was standing before the table with notepad in hand.

Camille perused the menu quickly and then said, "I'll have some rice and peas with oxtail. And," she scanned the menu again, "a serving of sweet plantains on the side. With a glass of white wine, please."

Harry ordered curry goat with rice and peas and a hefty bowl of mannish water soup.

"I'll pay for this," Camille whispered. And when he would have objected, she said firmly, "You have to give up this nonsense of wanting to pay each time we go anywhere. You don't have a job, for goodness' sake, and there's no point in pretending that you have stacks of money. We both know that you don't."

Harry leaned forward. "OK. You pay then. If you really want to." He slid a hand beneath the table and gently rubbed the length of her thigh. "Feel like a quickie?" he asked, wicked lights dancing in his eyes.

Camille grabbed his hand and tried to still its movement up and down her leg. "No," she said in a fierce whisper. "We can't. Not here."

"Aw, come on," Harry teased. "We could slip into the women's bathroom, lock the door. No one would be any the wiser."

Camille chuckled. It was a tempting idea. But she had to exercise some restraint. "Not here," she said again. "Maybe when we get back to . . ." But her voice petered out as she realized that she no longer had his attention. He was staring at a woman who had just walked in the door.

Camille touched him on the arm. "Something the matter?"

Harry looked at her, and the expression on his face made Camille ask in alarm, "What's wrong?"

"Nothing. Nothing really. I just don't want that woman to see us here."

Camille looked at the woman again. She seemed perfectly harmless, dressed in her work clothes. Maybe Harry had scammed some money off of her. A frown darkened Camille's eyes. Or maybe this was one of his women.

"Do you want to leave?" she asked with tight lips.

Harry shielded his face with a hand as the woman looked around for a place to sit. What was his assistant doing in a place like this in the middle of the day? Damn. She had seen him.

"Well," and Camille sat back in the booth, "seems like she's coming over." Whatever fireworks were in the offing, she would handle.

Nora smiled broadly. "Oh, hello, sir. How are you?"

"Fine. Fine." Harry nodded. And he gave her a steady look and hoped that she would understand that he wanted her to make herself scarce.

"I'm eating alone," she said, and waited for an invitation to join her boss. Her eyes flickered over Camille and iced by just a bit. Another one of his floozies, no doubt. Nora had suspected that he might be involved with another woman since he hadn't come into the office in weeks.

"Enjoy your meal then," and the expression on Harry's face sent her on her way.

Camille had watched the interplay between the woman and Harry with interest. "She called you sir," she said after a moment of silence. "And she totally ignored me. Why is that?"

Harry shrugged. "I have no idea."

"Is she someone you're dating?"

Harry laughed. "No. No. She's just someone I know. That's all."

Camille looked at the woman again. "Well, whoever she is, she was none too pleased to see me with you."

Harry had a long swallow of water and put the glass back on the table. "You know you're the only woman I'm seeing at the moment."

His comment managed to distract her. "Am I?"

He held her hand and kept an eye on Nora at the same time. "You know that. What's this all about?"

"Well, you've never really said that before. And we've never discussed it, either."

Harry cracked a knuckle, flexed his fingers. "Well, you are the only one. You're my girl. And I'm not seeing anyone else, OK?"

His response pleased her, and when their order came on steaming plates, she tucked into the oxtail and rice and peas with hearty enthusiasm.

Harry watched her eat, and as she bent her head to place another forkful of rice and peas in her mouth he came to a decision. This game he'd been playing with her had gone on long enough. Summer was right. He had to end it now. It had been a fool-hardy thing to do in the first place.

Camille looked up to find his eyes on her. "Not eating your food? I thought you said you were starving."

Harry picked up his knife and fork and began to eat. It wasn't right, playing with her in this way. He would tell her the truth about everything, when they got back home.

Chapter Twenty-four

Camille stripped off her panty hose and placed them on a hanger in the little closet. She had promised him that she would stay the night, so she had brought a change of clothes and all of her toiletries with her. There was nothing that she could do about the toilet situation, so if she felt the urge to go during the night, she would just have to go out to the shed in back.

"You know Summer's pregnant, right?" she asked now.

Harry appeared in the doorway to the bedroom. "Pregnant? Jeez. That should really go down well with Amanda."

"Amanda may be next, for all I know. I had a little talk with her a week or so ago. There are certain herbs you can take . . . and techniques you can follow."

Harry bent an elbow against the door frame. "What are you, the 'how to get pregnant' guru?"

She slipped out of her skirt and hung that up, too. "I know a few things."

Harry chuckled. "As long as you don't get pregnant yourself, I'm fine with the whole thing."

He came to stand beside her and he turned her to face him. This was probably the last night that they would spend together, and he wanted it to be perfect. He would tell her about everything in the morning.

He unbuttoned her blouse with careful fingers, making sure that the tiny pearl buttons did not come off in his hands. When he was through with the last one, he ran the flats of his hands up the run of her rib cage and over the mounds of her breasts.

Camille drew a shuddering breath. This man drove her crazy. How far she had come from just two months ago. How much she had changed. Or had she really? Maybe this had always been her true self. But she was happy, though. Happy that she was no longer that shallow, ridiculous person, who judged men by what they possessed instead of by who they really were.

She closed her eyes and surrendered herself to him as he whispered, "Let me give you a massage."

She lay flat on the mattress and let him remove her undergarments. She felt him come to kneel beside her and sighed in supreme satisfaction as his hands began to slowly knead her tired muscles. He moved slowly around her neck and then down across her shoulder blades to the small of her back. She made a contented sound and he asked in a husky whisper, "You like that?"

"Uhmm." She was several degrees beyond speech now.

He turned her on her side and ran his hands along the dip of her waist.

"Cam," he said. And Camille opened her eyes. It was the first time he had ever shortened her name.

"Yes . . . ?"

"No matter what happens, I want you to know that," he kissed her on the side of the neck, "I've really enjoyed spending this time with you."

"Uhm," she agreed. "Tell me later. Love me now."

And he did. Over and over again until finally, totally exhausted, they slept.

Chapter Twenty-five

In the morning, Harry was the first one to come awake, and he lay back on his arms, staring up at the ceiling and listening to the day come alive. How should he tell her? What words could he use to help her understand why he had done what he had done? She wouldn't understand, of course. She would scream at him. Call him every name in the book. She wouldn't understand that he had done it for her own good.

He sighed and then grabbed his phone as it began to ring. He spoke into the receiver, listened, and then said, "OK, I'll wake her."

He touched her on the shoulder. Shook her gently. "Camille?"

She yawned widely and said a very sleepy, "Uhm?"

Harry shook her again. "Camille? Wake up, sweetheart. Something's happened."

Camille came awake slowly. She opened eyes that were flushed a gentle pink. She glanced at her watch, sighed. "Why are you waking me up so early?"

Harry stroked the side of her face. "It's Lola."

Camille smiled. "On the phone? Why's she calling me so early? And how'd she know where to find me?"

"No, no," Harry said as gently as he could. "That was Summer on the phone. She was calling to let you know that something's happened to Lola."

A flush of fear ran through Camille, and she sat bolt upright, all traces of sleep gone. "What do you mean, something's happened to Lola? What's happened to her? What?" And at the expression on his face she shook her head and said, "No. . . ." Then stronger, "No. She's not . . . She can't be . . ."

"Her husband, Chaz, just called Summer. Her plane's gone missing."

Camille blinked numbly at him. Nothing was getting through to her at all. Nothing was making any form of sense. Lola St. James was a survivor. She'd survived everything in her life. Built herself up from absolutely nothing. She was a damn tough chick.

Camille sucked in a tight breath. "What do you mean, her plane's gone missing? How could it go missing?" Her voice ended in a little shriek.

Harry tried to hold her, but she pulled away. She stood and began to dress in a desperate manner, pulling on her clothes in brisk dragging movements. Shoes. Blouse buttoned the wrong way. Pants back to front.

"Let me help you," Harry said as she continued to

struggle with the clothes. "Take it easy. Take it easy. Let me help you."

Camille drew a shuddering breath and dashed a hand against the hot tear that trailed the length of a cheek. "She's OK," she told him. "Lola's not easy to kill. She's OK. They haven't found the plane yet, right?"

"Right," Harry said, and he undid the buttons on her blouse and refastened them the right way.

"That means that she could be alive."

Harry nodded. "There's still hope." He dragged her pants down and had her step into them again the right way.

She rested a hand on his back while Harry fiddled with her shoes, and he felt the tremble in her limbs.

"She'll be OK, honey," he promised Camille as the shaking grew worse. "She'll be OK."

"I've gotta go find her," she said. "She's all I have. Everyone else is gone. I've gotta go find her. She can't have left me. God wouldn't let that happen, right? He wouldn't let that happen."

Harry continued to mutter soothing things to her as he brushed her hair and scraped the long fall of it back behind her ears. "We'll take the Champagne jet," he said. "Don't worry; we'll find her. We'll find her."

Camille broke then and began to sob. "It's because of me that this has happened. I put a lot of bad stuff out into the universe, and now it's all coming back to me. Oh God."

Harry got her to sit down while he hustled into his clothes. When he was through with that, he picked up his cell phone and dialed.

"Nick," he said as soon as the phone was answered. "I need the jet. Camille's got an emergency." He listened and nodded. "We'll go straight to the private strip then. . . . Right. . . . OK. I'll see you."

He hurried her from the house, down the stairs, and into the Jeep.

"We have to hurry," she said in a broken and forlorn manner.

Harry started the engine with a roar. "We're hurrying, honey. We're hurrying. The plane'll be waiting for us when we get there. It'll take us maybe a half an hour to get to the private strip, so just sit back and pray, OK?"

Camille closed her eyes as they bumped down the rough track to the road. She tried to remember old prayers from her childhood, but suddenly none of them seemed very appropriate.

She looked across at Harry and saw him through a veil of tears. He wasn't a bum after all. He was a good, kind man who could be relied upon in a crunch. She closed her eyes again and prayed. *Lola. Lola. Lola. Please be safe. Please be all right. What will I do without you? What will you do without me?*

They'd been friends for such a long time. All their lives, really. They'd grown up together. She pressed a trembling finger to her nose. She wouldn't cry. She wouldn't cry. She wouldn't cry. Lola was all right.

Harry's cell phone rang again, and Camille jumped violently, and she turned to look at Harry with wide staring eyes.

"OK," He nodded. "OK. . . . Yes. She's right beside me. . . . No, I'll tell her. It's best."

Camille's heart pounded so heavily in her chest, it hurt. "What?" It was the only word that could make it beyond her trembling lips.

"They've found the plane."

Camille made a gasping sound. "Is she . . . is she . . . ?" She couldn't bring herself to even say it.

"They don't know yet. A rescue party has set off for the site of the crash. The plane went down in bad weather, somewhere just outside of Colorado."

Camille knit her fingers together. "She'll be OK," she muttered. "You don't know Lola. You don't know what she's like. She's a fighter."

Harry felt a deep surge of love flow through him at the expression on Camille's face. Damn it all to hell. Why did this have to happen to her? Hadn't she lost enough? Wouldn't she lose even more when he told her the truth about himself? Why was life so messed up?

They arrived at the private airstrip in just under half an hour, and as promised, the plane was waiting. Camille was surprised to see Nicholas on the

tarmac speaking to the pilot and even more surprised when Nicholas came over and handed them
both their passports.

"Summer found them," he said, and he held
Camille's hand in his for a moment. "Don't worry.
Everyone's praying for you."

Harry cuddled Camille in his arms the entire
flight across to the U.S. She had been too worried to
eat anything more than a few grapes. And as they
circled over Dulles, waiting for clearance to land,
she looked down at the hazy landscape and prayed
again that Lola be all right. She just had to be. She
just had to be.

They landed on schedule, and Chaz, Lola's husband, was waiting to pick them up. As soon as
Camille made it off the plane and into the car, she
hunted Chaz's face with her eyes, looking for any
sign of bad news.

Harry shook Chaz Kelly's hand and asked in a
discreet manner, "Anything yet?"

Chaz, who gave Harry the impression of being a
very solid and dependable kind of guy, said, "Nothing yet. But we're hopeful."

Camille lay back against the seats and left the
talking to Harry. She couldn't deal with anything
more at the moment. But she was very seriously im-
pressed by the way Harry was handling everything.
It was almost as though he were accustomed to jet-
ting about the world at a moment's notice. And he
didn't seem out of his element at all.

"Where are we going?" she asked Harry about fifteen minutes into the journey.

Harry massaged her shoulders. "We're going to go back to Lola and Chaz's place to wait for news. You try to sleep a little. I'll wake you when we're nearly there."

Chapter Twenty-six

Word came at eight thirty that night, and when Harry came into the bedroom that Chaz had given them and told her the news, Camille broke down and sobbed. Harry held her as she cried and mumbled over and over again, "Thank God. Oh, thank God. She's safe. She's safe."

"She's pretty badly banged up," Harry told Camille, "so they're medevacing her back to Georgetown Memorial."

Camille absorbed all of this. "But she'll live, right? She's not in any danger?"

"She'll live," Harry consoled her.

Camille swallowed and gathered herself. Lola would need a bag of things. Nightgowns. Underwear. Toiletries. Other things.

"I'll go pack her a bag now."

"OK," Harry nodded. "They say she should be at the hospital here in Maryland at around ten o'clock tonight. So we may not be able to see her until tomorrow."

"That's OK," Camille said. "Perfectly OK." And a surge of happiness filled her.

She looked in on Jamie, Chaz and Lola's little boy, and then went off to pack the bag. The child had been fast asleep, probably worn out from all of the excitement.

Harry was watching TV when she returned with the roll-away bag. He sat up when she came in, flicked off the TV set, and asked, "All done?"

"All done," Camille told him, and with such happiness in her eyes that Harry got up to give her a long, hard hug.

They were at the hospital within the hour, and Camille was waiting with her nose pressed up against the glass when the medevac helicopter flew in. She took a deep, filling breath at the sight of it hovering just above the helipad atop the hospital's surgical tower.

"She's here," she said to Harry and Chaz, and Harry came across from one of the waiting room chairs to hold her.

It was another hour before a doctor came out to see them and Camille listened while nibbling on the edge of a finger as they were told the extent of Lola's injuries. Broken arm. Broken leg. Fractured pelvis. Possible internal injuries. She was going right into surgery, so they would not be able to see her until the next day.

"Have you gotten ahold of Annie?" Camille asked Chaz as soon as they were alone again. Annie was more like a mother than a housekeeper to Lola, and if she heard the news of the crash on TV, there was no telling how that might affect her.

"She's on her way back from New York. She was out there visiting one of her children," Chaz told Camille. "She's holding up OK. But you know Annie. She's worried."

"We'll sleep here then, honey?" she asked Harry. She couldn't bear to go back to the house. She wanted to stay with Lola a little while longer.

Harry wrapped a warm arm about Camille. "We'll stay."

They passed the night curled up in uncomfortable straight-backed chairs. Camille tried to sleep but found that she couldn't, so she lay against Harry with her head nestled beneath his chin. And she tried to think of happy things. Jamaica. Adam and his love for bedtime stories. Amber and her puppies. Summer, a great new friend. Amanda and Nicky. Harry. Always Harry.

The night passed slowly. And since no one came out to give them any news, Camille assumed that things were going well.

At 8:00 a.m., Harry went to the nurses' desk to check and was told that Lola was resting comfortably in her room and would be available for visits from close family and friends only, sometime later in the afternoon.

Harry went to the cafeteria and brought Camille back some hot coffee and muffins and then sat to chat quietly with Chaz, who seemed about ready to collapse right there.

At two o'clock in the afternoon, a nurse came out to tell them that they could go in to see the patient now, but that their visit would have to be a short one. Camille was raring to go, but Harry whispered, "Let her husband go in to see her first."

The wait was unbearable, but finally Chaz came back out and beckoned them in. "She's a little woozy," he warned them. "Morphine and the after-effects of surgery. So, she might not recognize you."

Camille rushed ahead of them both, pushed open the room door, and covered her mouth with a hand. God, Lola was really banged up. A leg was in a cast and was attached to some sort of pulley mechanism. Her arm was in a cast. She had bandages around her head and around her chest.

Camille approached the bed on slightly shaky legs. "Lola? Lola honey?"

The patient in the bed turned her head slowly in the direction of her voice. "Cam?" she croaked.

Camille bent over her. "It's me. What are you do-ing hiding out here in the hospital when there are re-ally sick people out there?"

Lola's lips turned upward in a slight smile. "Don't make me laugh," she said softly. "I hurt like hell."

Camille gently stroked Lola's hair. "How are you feeling?"

Lola grimaced. "I'll be up and on my feet again in a week," she joked.

Camille chuckled. This was so like Lola. Always raring to go.

"What are you doing here anyway?" Lola asked, her voice cracking with the strain it took to pull coherent sound from her throat.

"Chaz called to say that your plane was missing. So, I came. I knew that no plane crash could . . ." and she wiped a tear from her eye, ". . . could snuff you out."

"It almost did," Lola told her. "I had to claw my way out of the wreckage, and away from the plane. I don't know; maybe that's what saved me."

Camille held her good hand, pressed it against her cheek, and said, "Thank God. Thank God."

Lola tried to turn her head to look at the men standing quietly in the shadows of the room. "Who's that over there?" she asked Camille.

Harry came forward to say, "You gave us all a scare."

And Lola looked at Camille. "Harry?" she asked.

Camille nodded. "Harry. Harry Britton."

Lola squeezed Camille's hand and whispered, "I like him."

Chapter Twenty-seven

Camille and Harry stayed in Maryland until Lola turned the corner in her recovery. She was released from the hospital after two weeks but was left in the care of a very capable home-care nurse. Annie fussed over Lola even more than the nurse herself, checking on her constantly to make sure that she was still breathing.

When Camille finally decided to return to Jamaica, Lola called her over to her bedside and said, "Listen to me, girl. If you do nothing else in your life, I want you to marry that man."

Camille grinned at her friend. The old Lola St. James was back. "He has to ask me first."

"He'll ask you." Lola smiled. "Can't you see the way he looks at you?" She wiggled her eyebrows. "And I know he can't keep his hands off you."

Camille kissed her on the cheek. "I'm thinking of just staying on in Jamaica for a while."

Lola rolled her eyes. "But of course you have to stay. Isn't Mr. Sexy Harry Britton there?"

"Uhm," Camille agreed. "But what about all of my stuff here? My car? My place?"

"I'll take care of everything."

"And what about you? I won't be able to see you every day. It won't be the same."

Lola shifted her broken arm. "Well, Chaz has always wanted to live in a warm country. So, who knows? Maybe we'll move there."

Camille went away with a happy feeling. Maybe everything would work out. Maybe she and Harry would make it together. Lola was usually right about things, and this was one time that Camille hoped that she was dead-on.

The trip back to Jamaica was quick, and before long they were trundling away from the airstrip in the black Jeep. Camille took a deep, luxuriant breath. It was good to be back. It was good to be finally home.

Camille looked at Harry and tried to read his face. He had been so quiet the entire trip over.

"Something bothering you?" she asked him now.

He gave her a distracted look. "I have something to tell you that you're not going to like. I'd meant to tell you weeks ago, but then this whole thing with Lola going missing cropped up, and you had too much on your plate."

Camille's heart began to beat in slow and heavy thumps. He was going to break up with her. She could hear it in his voice. "What do you want to tell me?"

"I'll tell you when we get back to my place."

And for the rest of the ride into Ocho Rios, Camille had to be satisfied with that. She was beginning to know her way around now, so when he passed Champagne Cove and kept going, she turned to look behind them and then asked, "Haven't we passed your house?"

"No," he said, and continued to drive toward Ocho Rios.

In a few minutes he was pulling up to a row of luxury condominiums. He pulled the Jeep into a space, cut the engine, and got out. Camille unbuckled herself and followed him.

"Where are we?" she asked when he began to climb the stairs to Condo 105.

Harry fit the key in the lock, turned it, and opened the door.

"I live here," he said once she was inside the condo. Camille looked at him and then laughed. "What do you mean, you live here? How could you afford to live here?"

Harry took her by the shoulders and sat her down on a comfy sofa. "Remember I said that I had something to tell you?"

Camille nodded, still not understanding what was going on, but sure that he was playing a joke of some sort on her.

"Well, this is what I wanted to tell you. I'm not who you think I am."

Camille tried to joke. "You mean you're really a woman?"

He didn't laugh at her feeble attempt at humor. "I mean I'm not a beach bum. I don't live in that house by the sea." He stopped, drew breath. "I'm a lawyer by profession. I'm the only son of the current Guyanese prime minister. I went to university in Britain. I am not poor. In fact, I'm what they call dirty, stinking, filthy rich."

Camille blinked at him. Had he suddenly gone stir-crazy? What was he talking about? Not only did he want her to believe that he was wealthy, but that he was also what? The son of a prime minister? And a lawyer, too?

Maybe he was ill. A sudden thought occurred to her. "Are you a diabetic?" she asked. She'd heard many a story of diabetics going into some sort of a confused state when their blood sugar dropped to dangerous levels.

Harry gave her a firm look. "I am not a diabetic. Or crazy, either. Let me show you something." And he got up to rustle about in a drawer. "Here's my law school diploma." He thrust it beneath her nose.

She took the leather-bound document, looked it over. It seemed real enough. And it had his name on it.

"OK," she said, "if you're a lawyer and whatever else you just said, how come your good friends the Champagnes don't know that you are?"

Harry sighed. "Of course they know who I am. I work for them as a lawyer."

Camille stood. She'd had just about enough of this. "You're a damned liar," she told him, her voice beginning to tremble. "And I don't know what kind of scam you're running now, but whatever it is, I want no part of it."

She turned to storm out of the condo, but Harry caught her by the door. "Let's go to the Internet then, OK? I couldn't have fake info there, right?"

He pulled her over to the computer, sat her down. "I'll do a search for Harry Britton, Guyana." He punched in the words with deft fingers. And within seconds, a long list of links was displayed.

"Let's have a look at this one. See what it says?" He pointed at the screen.

Camille read: *Prime minister's son visits Guyana.*

Her eyes darted down to the next line: *Harry Britton graduates with honors from Cambridge University.*

She kept reading. Line after line after line. And as she did, she grew colder and colder and colder.

By the time she was finished, she felt like a solid block of ice. It had all been a lie then. Everything had been a lie. Everything. That horrible house. The shack in the back. The mattress on the floor. All props? Nothing real? All to make a fool out of her? And the Champagnes knew? Everyone knew?

She looked up at him and in a very calm voice asked, "Why did you do this?"

Harry tried to hold her hand, but she snatched it away. "I'm sorry," he said. "But I thought you were a gold digger, so I—"

She stood. "You wanted to hurt me. And you got your friends to help." She could see it clearly now. What a fool she was. Maybe there was something wrong with her brain. First the thing with Anthony, now this. Would life never stop hurting her?

"You got me good," she said in a sad little voice. "I've got to give you that. You got me good. Well, I guess this is good-bye," and she looked at him with such hurt in her eyes that Harry actually felt a physical pain in his chest.

"Not good-bye," he said. "I want you with me. Always."

Camille laughed in a hard and bitter way. "If you were the last man on earth, I still wouldn't have you. Amanda Champagne was right about you. You are a bastard. Through and through."

She slammed out of the condo and ran blindly down the stairs. What an embarrassment. What an absolute embarrassment. To think of all of the things she had said to him. How he must have laughed at her. God.

She began to run when she heard Harry's voice behind her. Where could she go now? She couldn't go back to the Champagnes'. Not after this.

Harry ran down the stairs, taking them two at a time, and sprinted after her. She was going to take him back, and what's more, she was going to marry him, too.

He tackled her from behind and they both fell in a tangle of limbs.

"Leave me alone, you . . . you freak, you. I don't want you."

Harry struggled to still her arms and grimaced as a knee went dangerously close to his groin. "You want me," he said. And he pressed a kiss to her face. "You want me." Another kiss fell on the tip of her nose. "You love me. And what's more, I love you, too."

Camille stopped struggling. "I don't love you. You're just a conceited, lying piece of—"

"You don't love me?" he cut her off. "Look me in the eye and say that again."

He stroked a hand against the curve of her thigh, and a shudder went through Camille.

"Tell me."

"I don't."

"So that means that you won't marry me then?"

Camille blinked at him. Marry him? Now, that was a different matter entirely.

"You want to marry . . . me?"

"I do. So what do you say?"

"I don't know," Camille said, and she squealed when he smacked her on the butt. "I'll have to think about it. Really."

He kissed her again. "Enough time?"

"Not yet," she said breathlessly.

He kissed her again, this time with complete thoroughness.

"What about now?"

Camille grabbed his head between her two hands and said, "OK, you lying vagabond. I'll marry you. But you'd better not ever pull a stunt like this one again."

Epilogue

One Year Later

Camille reached across to squeeze Lola's hand as the low-slung limousine swept down the narrow roads toward beautiful St. George's Cathedral. It was still completely unbelievable that she was in Guyana. So much had happened in the past year. She and Harry had moved in together in Jamaica, and she, with his strong support, had plunged right into the working world. It had been hard at first, getting used to the routine. But very soon into it, she'd found that working every day for a living was nowhere near as bad as she'd always thought it would be. Sure, she had to get up at six-thirty every morning and put in a full day of sweat and toil, but it was good, rewarding work, and for the first time in years, she felt really good about herself.

Three months after Harry had proposed to her, he took her to Guyana to meet his sister and his parents. And although she had been highly nervous

about the whole thing, they had welcomed her into
the family in a way that had touched her deeply. She
hadn't expected them to like her. She had even been
secretly afraid that Harry's father might put an end
to the entire thing. That he might tell his son that
she, Camille Roberts, was not the kind of woman
that a man like Harry should marry. But she had
been wrong about that, and wrong about almost
everything. The country's beauty had struck her too,
and many mornings during their brief stay, she had
woken with the same prayer on her lips. *Please let it
not be a dream. Please let it not be a dream.* It was
so impossible, so unbelievable that everything and
more that she had pursued with such cold calcula-
tion in years past had come to her in such an easy
and effortless manner. Did she deserve it? Did she
deserve a man like Harry? Why had life been so
good to her?

She sniffled and rubbed a hand beneath her nose
as a fresh rush of tears came to her eyes.

Lola peered at her through the veil and said in a
tolerant manner, "Crying again? Come on, girl,
you've got to stop all that. We're almost at the
church now."

Camille gave her friend a watery smile. Lola was
right. She had to pull herself together. She did deserve all that had happened to her. And she would
make Harry a good wife. An excellent wife. And
best of all, she would give him children. Lots of
them. Just as they both wanted. It was so funny how

life had a way of working out sometimes. And to think that because of cold avarice, she might have actually married a man like Anthony Davis. Every time she thought about that, a cold shudder ran right through her.

"OK, we're here," Lola said as the big car pulled to a slow stop directly before the mouth of the church. "And remember, don't walk too fast. I'm still a little stiff from the accident."

Camille's heart hammered in her chest. *Lord have mercy* but there were a lot of people there. It was almost as though the entire country had turned out just to see her marry Harry.

"Ready?" Lola asked, beaming at her.

Camille sucked in a breath and nodded. "Ready."

Lola fluffed her veil and said, "OK then. Let's go get you married."

Camille stepped from the car, and as she appeared, the crowd applauded loudly. She tried to smile and nod at them all, but found that her lips were trembling just a little too much for that. She felt Lola directly behind her, and then caught sight of little Amber Champagne, all decked out in a beautiful peach-colored gown, standing at the mouth of the church. Her heart picked up and began to hammer in her chest as the organ went smoothly into the wedding march.

"Come on, girl, you're almost there. You're almost there," came Lola's voice from just behind.

Camille could see them all standing at the church

door now. Her bridesmaids. Summer. Amanda. Alana. And Annie. A sob caught in the back of her throat. *If only her mother could have been here too.*

As she entered the church with Amber and Adam Champagne leading the way, the entire crowd rose to its feet. Harry's father peeled away from the crowd, and offered her his arm. And she swept down the aisle to where they were all waiting. The groomsmen were dressed in immaculate black tuxedoes with brilliant white shirts. All of the Champagne men. Nicholas. Gavin. Mik. Rob. Her eyes took in them all, and then settled on Harry. Dear, darling Harry. Standing there, looking so tall and handsome and nervous at the same time. Camille turned her head to smile at his mother as she passed. And the older woman returned her smile and gave her an encouraging nod.

And suddenly, the long walk was at an end, and she was there, standing beside Harry. Holding his hand. Looking up into his eyes. And it was wonderful. Magnificent. Fantastic. . . .